FLYBOY

Top Flight: A Fighter Pilot Romance

SOPHIA SUMMERS

Read all Top Flight Fighter Pilot Romances

Ace
Bear
Flyboy
Mustang

Read all books by Sophia Summers

JOIN HERE for all new release announcements, giveaways and the insider scoop of books on sale.

A whole series of Holiday Romances. Click Here.

Read all the books in The Swoony Sports Romances
Hitching the Pitcher
Falling for Centerfield
Charming the Shortstop
Snatching the Catcher
Flirting with First
Kissing on Third

Her Billionaire Royals Series:
The Heir
The Crown
The Duke
The Duke's Brother
The Prince
The American
The Spy
The Princess

Her Billionaire Cowboys Series:
Her Billionaire Cowboy
Her Billionaire Protector
Her Billionaire in Hiding
Her Billionaire Christmas Secret
Her Billionaire to Remember

Her Love and Marriage Brides Series
The Bride's Secret
The Bride's Cowboy
The Bride's Billionaire

Chapter 1

Colton, call sign *Flyboy*, returned home to Texas on a rare break from his Top Flight pilot teams to check on his dad. He'd had a little scare when his dad went in for testing after strange bloodwork, but the strong eighty-year-old man had been cleared of any serious issues. Colton would spend a couple more days with his parents and his brothers, who'd come into town for the rodeo, then he was off on the next assignment.

He urged his horse to a gallop. He and Pepper flew across his parents' back pasture. Not quite like an F-16, but there was still something about being up on a horse that brought most things in his life back into neat little lines where they belonged. He wasn't usually appreciative of neat little lines, and he avoided labels and boxes. He had barely made it through the military with an honorable discharge, but not because he was trouble. He'd served well and had medals to prove it, but they sat in his top drawer here at home at his parents' house. He steered his horse toward their favorite jump over a half-broken fence at the edge of the creek toward the back of the property. Maybe it was still there.

Pepper seemed to know where they were going, and Colton let the horse have his head. They took off even faster. He smiled so long his teeth hurt, and then they flew over the fence, cleared the creek, and kept racing out across the field on the other side. His horse leaped over smaller logs and rocks, anything in their way. Colton rose up in his saddle and put his arms out. The horse hit the steep upward climb on the hill in front of them as if it was nothing. They hadn't been up to the top in over a year.

As soon as they reached the top, Colton felt his phone vibrating in his chest pocket. It was the Top Flight phone. Calls on that phone tended to be important, or if not that, urgent at the least. He dismounted and let Pepper wander.

"Ace," he said into the phone with a smile.

"Fly. Good to hear your voice, man. It's been a while." It was his friend and the reason he sat on a board of four people who ran the Top Flight training programs.

They'd been doing most of their meetings over Zoom, but those had been nothing but business. "Yeah, yours too. Where are you right now?"

"Amazon Rainforest. But I'm coming home to Virginia so I can gear up and run my next group."

"Amazon, huh? Did you get a good look at anything I'm going to be seeing while we're down there?"

"No, nothing like that. These villages, dude. They're like nothing even I've ever seen."

"You figuring it out?"

"Yeah. So far."

Ace spent half the year working on Top Flight assignments and the other half doing humanitarian work for underprivileged children. If Colton had to guess, the village he'd just left now had a well for clean water and the new workings of a school.

"That's awesome, man. So, I'm glad you called. I have some questions about my assignment."

"So do I."

Colton walked to the edge of the ridge to look out over the whole valley in front. "Shoot."

"So while I was down there, I made some phone calls, and Brazil only has two planes."

"What?"

"Right. And a team of fifteen pilots to train."

Colton frowned. "I could do that by myself."

"Or maybe with just one other from Top Flight."

"Right." Colton shook his head. "Should we talk about it at our board meeting?"

"Yep, but before I brought it up there, I thought I'd mention it to you . . . you know, give you a heads up so you could think about it."

"Thanks, man." He knew who he wanted on his team. Ivy Hatfield. But why did he want her? That was the question that had him out here pounding the miles around his parents' home. Was she qualified? Certainly. Would he enjoy working with her? That wasn't the question that most concerned him. Something about her getting under his skin in an uncomfortable, itchy-but-good way, hung around in his head. And then there was the question about whether or not he should scratch the itch.

But as they began their Zoom meeting a few days later, Ace surprised him by not saying anything about the missions at the beginning like he usually did. Colton liked their board meetings. He was always reminded what a cool thing they'd all started. A pilot training program. Skills and consulting offered all over the world.

"Ridley! How are things with you? How's the little squirt?" Ace grinned.

"We're doing great," Ridley answered. "She's such a trooper about all this, really. But what about you? It's been a long time. How's the jungle?"

"It's amazing. We've got the village all squared away. We have three new wells drilled and a school up and working, as well as education on newborn resuscitation and basic sanitation."

Just as Colton had thought. Of course he'd taken care of all of that. How would it be to be Ace? Colton was good at things too, just one thing at a time.

"That's awesome, dude," Ridley said.

"What about you, Mustang?" Ace twirled a pencil, leaning back in his chair. Zoom was fine, but Colton wanted to sit in a real room with each of the board sometime.

"I'm ready for another mission, that's what."

"And I have the four we've chosen ready for you," Ace said. "But before we go through our pilots and choose teams, there's something else we need to address."

That sounded ominous. He tried to get a read on Ace, but he just couldn't tell all that much through a Zoom chat image.

"We had a letter of complaint."

"A what?" Colton couldn't remember there ever being a letter of complaint.

"Yes. There's really nothing for it. I'm not sure what to think, so I'll just read it."

Was he taking this letter seriously? Or was he laughing inside? Looking at the now intense expressions of the others, Colton shifted in his seat at the dining room table and leaned closer as if peering into the screen would help him figure things out.

Ace unfolded a piece of paper. "This is from Ivy Hatfield."

Colton's heart hammered inside. And a knot in his stomach grew.

"I'll skip to the good stuff." Ace cleared his throat. "Colton Bushman has proven overly aggressive in his efforts to teach the more challenging flying to pilots who lack experience. When he teaches, he is goaded on by their encouragement and creates an atmosphere of recklessness that is a danger not only to himself but to all our pilots. While I see that Top Fight wants to improve upon the training pilots may have received previously, I don't feel it is in anyone's best interest to create a team of pilots all over the world who take undue risks and potentially lose lives and expensive planes." Ace cleared his throat. "She goes on, for three pages. But that was the gist of what she continued to say in many different ways."

"Sounds like she's got a real bone to pick with you. Did you do a flyby and scare her one time or something?" Ridley shook his head.

"No, nothing like that at all. I can't figure out why she, of all people, would have written this. We've never worked together." Colton couldn't make up his mind about whether to be irritated, hurt, or amused.

"She's around. She sees you or hears of you." Amanda interjected, and her tone gave Colton pause.

"What are your thoughts, Mustang?"

5

"I think you need to let her see why you do what you do. Maybe you could explain your methods and theories to her." Her tone sounded a little too placating to Colton.

"Why should I have to talk at all about it? My actions speak for themselves. My history, the pilots I've trained. It can all stand on its own."

"I know you're an exceptional pilot. We know that. But it's so much easier for people to know you or understand you if you spell it out a little bit. None of us can read minds."

"Ace? Ridley?"

Ridley cleared his throat. "Might want to talk to her."

"None of you agree with her?"

Every one of them shook their heads.

"Honestly, Flyboy, we love it when you do your amazing maneuvers. No one can fly like you. Hands down. No one. And we know that. We trust you." Ace would always come through. And it sounded like the others didn't think he was a danger to pilots everywhere.

Colton shrugged. "Looks like Ivy Hatfield needs a little Flyboy education. So now I'm going to request for her to be on my team." Of course, he knew he was already planning to do just that, but they didn't need to know that, or that her words cut deeper coming from her than they would anybody else. He couldn't just shake them off. They were sticking to him in uncomfortable places.

Silence met him, and then Ridley shook his head. "That'll be something. Could I come just to watch the show?"

"I've got the popcorn." Amanda grinned.

Ace wiped laughter tears from his eyes. "Now, you know the four of us know what an asset you are to our team, but it seems we have yet to convince Ivy. Perhaps it would be best if you just give her a lot of room for a few months. What do you think?"

Colton shook his head. "No. I've convinced myself. I want her on my team. In Brazil."

"I don't know if that's such a good idea . . . did you hear what she said?"

"I heard it. And what better way to prove her wrong?"

He saw the hesitation on every one of their faces. "I know we need a smaller team, but I thought maybe Jed, Rocky, or Omar could come with us? Ivy seemed to get along well with all of them."

"I think a good consideration of any of those others is a great idea." Ace was still holding back support of asking for Ivy. Colton could read it all over his face.

"And Ivy." Colton didn't know what it was about her ridiculous letter of complaint, but her words—as off base as they were—had cinched his determination to ask for her on his Brazil team.

"Wait, are you serious?" Ace tried to study his face through the screen.

"I'm serious. Hey, don't worry about me. She'll be singing a whole new tune in no time. No one can resist my Texas charm for long."

"That might be the wrong approach . . . " Amanda didn't often mince words. She was careful with her tone, but Colton could see all over her face how bad an idea she thought it would be for Colton to ask for Ivy on his team.

"I'll address her concerns myself." Colton smiled.

"And just how will you do that?" Ridley had been quiet. Colton wondered what he thought.

"I'll call her. Ask her point-blank." Colton shrugged. "And then after I hear her reasoning about why I'm not qualified to lead this organization, you can let her know her next assignment."

"Colton." Amanda's smile gave him hope. "You're the fastest pilot we have. No one would ever dispute your contributions to the pilot world either. They're still studying your move at Top Gun, you know. But have you considered that there might be some truth to what she says?"

"Whoa. Now hold on, Mustang. We all have different theories about discipline and rule-following, and everybody's style is needed."

"It's true, Flyboy. None of us can argue with your record."

"Darn right. If it weren't for the Fly, things would have gone very differently in Afghanistan. Someone had to break the rules, and that someone was usually Colton. But I see your point. The Ivys in the world are important too."

Didn't have to tell him twice. He couldn't seem to get her out of his system. And he was hoping that being in such close quarters with the woman day in and day out would cure him of his interest, especially now that he knew she loathed him enough to write a three-page letter of complaint. He'd never seen two more highly incompatible people. And he obviously drove her to distraction.

He smiled.

Was that a good thing or a bad thing? But he had to convince the other three that working with Ivy was a good idea. "Okay, so here's how I see things. She obviously has a problem with me. Maybe I can learn something from her, and to be honest, maybe she can learn something from me. She's coming at me all wrong, and we all know it."

Was he just asking for trouble?

His attention wandered out to the fenced pastures

surrounding his home. He had one more day here and then it was off to Brazil, ahead of his team. "I want Ivy. I need her, anyway. I'm heading down to Brazil early. And she and either Omar or Jed can join me down there at the end of the week." It was hard to tell what everyone really thought about his opinions from a Zoom call.

"Let's talk about our other teams, then." Amanda seemed ready to let it go. Ridley hadn't said much, and he knew if Ace had a real problem, he'd hear about it, now and later.

But they moved on. The slide show of all their potential pilots started playing, and the Top Flight board of directors started picking out the best pilots for the teams they were each putting together.

Colton could never have guessed that their new idea, to gather discharged military pilots and put together an international training program, would have taken off the way it had. They had more work than time, more pilots applying to be a part of it every day, and a healthy income. When Ace had told him there was money to be made and that he could still get up in a plane now and then, Colton had jumped at the chance. There was nothing else to do with his life anyway. Everything lacked the thrill of being up in those planes; nothing felt as important as being deployed for his country.

Top Flight filled a lot of holes in his life.

And he was lonely. But so far, he hadn't found anything or anyone that could solve that problem. When he figured out what women really wanted, he was sure he'd also see, plain as day, that he wasn't it.

He hardly listened as the other three assigned the teams. When he logged off the call and stared at the names of those who would be on his team for the next four to six months, he didn't know if he really wanted what he'd fought for.

Ivy. Who hated him, apparently.

And Omar. He hadn't spelled it out to the others, but Omar was there to be a buffer between Ivy and him.

He rubbed his face. This was going to be some assignment.

Chapter 2

When Amanda told her she was being assigned to Flyboy's team, Ivy almost lost her cool . . . almost.

"Mustang."

"I know. Don't even say it. Well, okay, you can say it. I'll listen."

"I plan to tell Flyboy too. This feels like a cruel joke. I submit a formal complaint, and you guys put me on his team? All the frustrations of working with him aside, he knows I complained about him. He's bound to dislike the experience as much as I will."

"On the contrary. He asked for you. He was adamant about it."

Something inside did a little flip. "Why would he do that?" She shook her head. "Is this some joke to him?" Did he really want her on his team? That was crazy.

"He said you're the best pilot for the job. Maybe it was just a professional decision." Amanda was the best part of Top Flight in Ivy's opinion. She'd connected with her immediately, and the two often sat together when the testosterone in any room was thick.

"I can do this," Ivy told herself more than Amanda.

"Of course you can. Colton's a sweetheart. His heart is in the right place. Just remember there are lots of ways to reach the same goal."

Ivy sighed, said goodbye, and logged off the call. "The same goal. Do we have the same goal?" Her words hung in the air in her apartment. She reached for her bags and headed to the airport. Rio Grande do Sul, Brazil. It would be cold. She hadn't flown cold in a long time. And she didn't savor the experience.

But it would be an easy job—two planes, fifteen pilots. She'd be on the ground more often than not. With any luck, they would finish early.

And, Colton or not, she loved working for Top Flight. Once she'd been honorably discharged, she had looked for her purpose, looked for a place to fit in, but nothing else in life had been so comfortably regimented, so perfectly orderly as the military. So when she heard of opportunities at Top Flight, she jumped at the chance.

But nothing in life was ever exactly as you'd expect.

Still, she loved her job. Top Flight was easily the best thing to happen to her since the military. If the others wouldn't listen to her complaints and would then ask her to work with Colton as her team lead, then she would do it.

Colton. She shook her head and smiled in spite of herself. If he weren't so dang charming in an irresponsible, irritating, and unacceptable sort of way, this would be easier. He'd gotten away with this reckless behavior all these years because he could smile like no one else she'd ever seen, as if the whole sun beamed out through his eyes. Well. She would work with him. But she wasn't going to let that smile turn her into a sappy, soft, Colton follower.

He was dangerous. Plain and simple. In more ways than one. She shook her head and reminded herself that she knew what happened when pilots were dangerous. And no matter how it made her appear, no matter how much they all talked about her clipboard-carrying exactness to obedience, she knew the alternative, and she wasn't going there. And Colton couldn't either, not if a simple warning could do the trick.

The taxi dropped her off for curbside baggage, but she walked past with her no-nonsense carry-on and made her way through security. Not everyone could have their own jet. Not like Ace. Must be nice. She was pretty sure every member of the board of Top Flight was swiftly making their own millions. Her own salary was not too shabby. She lifted her chin. She could do this. She could work with an irresponsible man as her superior. She'd done it before.

When she landed in Brazil, the stark beauty of the mountains, the crisp air, and the lovely people did a lot to lighten her expectations and give her hope. This job certainly brought her to places she would never be otherwise. Rio Grande do Sul made up the very most southern tip of Brazil. Probably like most people, she'd always thought of Rio and hot beaches when she thought of Brazil.

The architecture as she drove through Puerto Allegre kept her eyes glued to the window. The driver was kind enough to point out churches and other sights in his remarkably clear English. "We have penguins and snow here in the south."

"Remarkable."

"Most people from other countries—they don't know that."

"I didn't either." She shivered even though she wasn't

cold as yet. The weather was mild. The sun was bright. The vegetation all around with full leaves seemed to indicate summer. Their road curved as they left the city and was lined with trees and her favorite flower bushes seemingly growing wild on the side of the road. "Hydrangeas."

"Oh, yes. They love our country. The big blooms are everywhere. Even my mother sometimes, she would cut them back."

"They're stunning." Light blues and pinks with the occasional deeper colors stretched on both sides of the road for as far as she could see. The flowers were as large as her head. She clicked a few photos with her phone. How often would she see something like this again?

"How long will you stay in our country, miss?"

"Six months, I think."

"Oh, that is wonderful. Then you will see the festivals. The German towns have their festivals, and the tourists love them." His smile grew. "You like our country. You stay so long."

"Yes, I'm here for work."

"Very good. We work down here in the south. We work hard. Not like the others in the north. Every day there's a party in the Bahia, did you know?" He shook his head like something so innocuous as daily parties was offensive to his understanding of the world.

Ivy smiled. "Sounds like a great place to visit."

"Visit." He shrugged. "It's true. The beaches are beautiful. You go visit there once, and you will be counting the moments until you come back to the south. Here you can see the beautiful beaches and the buildings and the mountains and also get all your work done." He nodded. Then they pulled up in front of a large home.

"Are we here?" She pulled up her phone to check the address. "Yes, looks like it." It was surrounded by a gate, and two large parrots sat on either pedestal in the front.

"They're gorgeous. Why don't they fly?"

"They're trained. Probably. I don't know." He didn't seem as intrigued or as excited to talk about the birds. "This house is a good one. I know the owner. She take care of you." He brought her bags to the front gate and clapped his hands. "*Oi de casa!*"

A window upstairs opened, and a smiling older woman in her fifties leaned her head out the window. "Oh, Roberto. Hello, Ivy. You must be my new guest?"

"I am. I think Mr. Bushman must have called to set this up?"

The house was white stucco, brilliant in the afternoon sun, which felt warm on her face in a pleasant way; the air was chillier than she expected.

"Yes, he did. Come on in. Roberto, please bring that woman's bags inside."

"For you, for her, I will do it. You are staying in the finest house in our city."

Ivy smiled. "It is beautiful." A large awning ran along the front, and the door was the brightest blue she had ever seen.

The woman opened it with another large, white-toothed smile, her curls piling around her face, tickling her forehead. She leaned in, kissing each of Ivy's cheeks. "*Bem vindo mi filha.*"

"Oh, *Obrigada.*" Ivy felt flustered for a moment. The charming welcome was so sincere, so full of happiness, and the kisses—she wasn't used to it, but it made her smile. "I'm Ivy Hatfield."

"Fatima. Everyone just calls me Fatima."

"Fatima. It's good to meet you. Thank you for having us."

"I was so happy to get the call. I denied every other rental request so that I could have the American pilots come stay at my house." She stepped back and indicated they should come in. "Roberto, once you put her bags in the yellow room, come into the kitchen for some *suco*."

Roberto's face wrinkled with a brilliant smile. "She makes the best *suco de Aracaju*." *Mmmm.*

"Come in, come in." She led the way into a bright and open front room. The windows were opened, no screens blocked their view.

Ivy let some of the tension tightening her shoulders release. "This is such a beautiful home."

"Oh, thank you. It's been in our family for five generations. Please make yourself comfortable. All the main rooms are open to our guests. Just the family rooms are private. The back yard is for your use, and you will notice a pretty path down the way there. If you go for a mile or so, you will see a waterfall."

"I'm sure I will be very comfortable here. Thank you."

"You're welcome. Now, you go, feel free to freshen up, rest, or whatever you like, dear. I'll bring up some refreshments in just a moment."

Ivy smiled and made her way to the back of the house and up a set of stairs. Her room sat in the back corner. It was large with a huge, soft-looking bed in the middle of the room against the back wall. Two windows overlooked the green rolling hills that seemed to stretch in every direction.

Her smile started small, but soon, she was rocking back and forth from heel to toe and grinning from ear to ear. A noise at her door turned her head, looking for her promised refreshment. "Fatima, this view. I could look all day . . ." She turned to congratulate her hostess.

But instead of Fatima, Flyboy stood in the doorway.

Her energy left her as quickly as it had come. "Oh."

"Hey." Flyboy nodded his head. "So, you're here and got settled in?"

"Just arrived, yes."

"Omar and I came together. He's down at the end of the hall that way."

She nodded.

"And I'm right next door."

She swallowed through a suddenly very dry mouth. She had nothing, no words, no thoughts beyond the fact that she'd sent a detailed letter to the whole board, including this man standing in front of her, explaining why he was a danger to any mission. And another glaring realization that Colton's hair was newly cut, and the military shave made his eyes look . . . different, and his jawline, sharper, thicker—or something —more handsome. The realization tickled something inside, something . . . pleasant. She blinked it away before it bloomed into . . . anything.

"Ok, great." Why was he still standing in her doorway? "We meet the pilots tomorrow?"

"Not for a couple of days, actually."

She tilted her head. "I thought your email said to arrive today, that we were under the wire?"

"Oh, well, no, not under the wire, but I thought it might be good for our team to get together ahead of time, get settled in, get to know the people, and . . . bond." He winked. Then he laughed. "It might be nice if we liked each other before we start this assignment."

Again, she found herself speechless for a moment, and then she shook her head. "Liked each other?"

"Yeah, I need a couple days to prove I'm not . . . what were the words? A danger to the team? And an embarrassment to the word pilot?"

She felt her face heat, but she refused to stand down. "I stand by my words, but I hope there isn't anything uncomfortable between us."

"Not at all. I just have my work cut out for me."

"Your work?"

"Yes, we can't work well together when you have such disheartening opinions about me. And I have a couple days to prove to you that I just might be a good pilot after all."

"I never said you weren't a good pilot." She looked away, flustered. "I . . . look. I don't want weird feelings, either. Let's just forget I said anything for the time being." She shrugged.

He shook his head. "Nope. We are going to address every one of those complaints."

She stepped closer, ready to talk him out of this ridiculous plan. "No, really. That is not necessary."

"Oh, but it is."

"Why?"

"I don't know. Except I can't have you over there thinking negative thoughts about me."

"What if I just tell you I'm not . . . thinking negative thoughts." Of all the ridiculous conversations.

"I'll know you're just trying to get out of it." He dipped his head and then smiled, a slow curl of his lips, the kind she shouldn't look at for too long. "Come on. Give me a chance." His eyes widened, and he turned a pleading, adorable expression in her direction.

She couldn't stop the smile that lifted one corner of her

mouth in return. But she covered it and said, "Of course. We have to work together. Let's make it as pleasant as possible."

The light in his eyes dimmed, but he nodded at her. "Good enough. Put on some comfortable hiking shoes."

"Pardon me?"

"Apparently, there's a waterfall we must see before another hour goes by."

Chapter 3

Colton did not congratulate himself that he'd found a way to spend the rest of the afternoon with Ivy, even if Omar would be joining them. He knew she was humoring him for professional reasons only. But whatever the reason, he was going to make the most of the time he had to prove his point. And what was his point? He shrugged into a lightweight sweatshirt. Who knew what his point was? Something didn't sit well, just under his skin, like a new itch, whenever he thought about Ivy not approving of him or his methods. There was absolutely more than one way to do things. And she was just about to get a crash course on Colton's way if he had anything to say about it. Once he'd done his best, if she still had the same opinions, then so be it. But . . . he wanted her to like him so much that he might one day see her smile at him, in just the right way.

He stepped out the front door, stretching his arms above his head. But today—these next two days—were all about fun. And if Colton could do anything, he could do fun.

Omar's frown, when he stepped out the door, made Colton laugh. "What is it?"

"It's not humid here."

"I'd think that was a good thing."

He grunted. Then he squinted up into the sun. "This is perfect weather. I feel like we're in San Diego."

"Well, then I see nothing you should be frowning about."

"This ain't frowning. This is my normal expression."

"He's right." Ivy stepped out to join them. "You should have seen him on the islands. Everything around us as beautiful as it gets, and Omar is over there frowning."

"Ivy." He pulled her in for a hug. Colton felt every part of his body bristle like a prickly pear cactus, while he watched the two of them embrace.

"It was hotter than any place needs to be and humid on top of it." He looked up at the sky. "But this. I could go to a lot of assignments with weather like this."

Omar was a good, solid, passionate sort of guy. The more missions he went on, the more the team wanted to use him. But if he kept hugging Ivy like they were the best pals in the world, Colton might not like him as much.

"Let's be off, then. We've got two days to appreciate the weather before we're stuck indoors." Colton led the way down a path to their left. He hummed to himself while the other two chattered together. At first, the path was wide, lined with grass and rocks, but the further on they went, the more dense the vegetation became. Soon the three of them were walking in a single file line. Thick underbrush rubbed against his legs and branches scratched at his arms, making him grateful for his sweatshirt.

After about thirty minutes, the path opened up again and then stopped at the edge of a huge rock outcrop overlooking a pool that splashed with a frothy foam as the towering plunge of the powerful torrent rushed downward. Mist refreshed Colton's face as he lifted his chin, eyes closed, into the spray of the falls that rose above them. Ivy came to stand beside him. "This is really incredible."

"It really is." He winked at her, peered down off the rocky ledge at the pool beneath them and then dove off.

Her scream behind him as he fell made him laugh. Then he shouted a great whoop of happiness to the nature all around them until his hands hit the water. He sunk into the cool depths and then swam to the surface. He looked up at the rock outcropping and laughed at Ivy's face, peering over the edge at him. He waved and then swam over to the side.

As he suspected, Ivy and Omar did not follow him down the same way. They made their way along the path. He could almost feel Ivy shaking her head in his direction.

Well, she needed to learn to relax a little bit.

And she thought he needed to act more responsibly. Well, he would keep trying to change her mind.

When they finally reached him, he was making his way across the rocks toward the falls. "Come on. There's supposed to be a cave behind here."

"Wait for us. I gotta do something first." Ivy's voice sounded excited enough that he turned. And to his amazement, she dove into the water. When she came up, he cheered.

She shook out her hair, her eyes sparkling up at him. "I was so hot after that climb. This feels nice."

"The water is chilly, but I imagine it feels just right."

She swam over to him and lifted her hands up on the rocks. He knelt down and offered her a hand just as Omar joined them. "I'm not getting in that. Who knows what kinds of things live in that water."

"This?" Ivy used his hand as leverage and stepped up beside him. She was surprisingly light.

"Wow, you're strong." The grin she sent his way was less guarded, almost impressed. She turned to Omar. "It's too cold for anything too terrible to live in there. You should try it. After that climb, it feels amazing."

Omar just grunted and then moved to step beneath the falls. "Did someone say we're going back behind here?" He skirted the edge, letting the water cascade down all around him. He shook his now-drenched hair.

"Yes. Follow me. There's a ledge." Colton followed along the left-hand side. Fatima had told him it led to a cave behind the falls. They were able to skirt the strongest force of the falls and hug the side of the rock cliff. Once past the front of the falls, he stepped up onto another ledge and then into a recess in the rocks. He turned as the others joined him, and they all stared at a sheet of water to their front.

"Wow, this is really cool." Ivy reached her hand out. The water powered into her palm. "That's so much stronger than it looks."

"It really is." Colton turned, his shoulder bumping Ivy's. "Oops. Excuse me."

The face she turned up to him was open, friendly. Hmm. Good. Progress. Her hair hung down around her in wet waves. Her clothes clung to her in ways he liked. And above all, she seemed as into this adventure as he was. "They say that the cave goes back a ways, and if we choose the right direction, it actually opens up back near the original path." He stepped closer to her and winked. "Or . . . buried treasure."

Omar snorted.

"Truth. They've never found it. But they say, long ago, there was a time everyone in the area was hiding all their belongings because of the robbers that plagued their land. And during that time, many forgot where they hid things. This place is crawling with ancient treasure. Says the rumors."

"Rumors?" Ivy's voice sounded amused, at least.

"Well, says Fatima."

She laughed. "Excellent. Well, we need to cross our fingers for some hidden treasures *and* the path back to the house."

"That's what I'm talking about. And dinner," said Omar.

"Fatima is our chef for the week as well."

"Wow, Flyboy," Ivy said, "this is a great set-up. How far away are we from the hangar and the airstrip?"

"It's just up the road. We can't quite walk, but Fatima has an old truck we can use." He shrugged. "Or the rental car."

"What's going to be the protocol with this group?" she asked. "Are we starting with the classroom group A, or are they more advanced? Were they able to complete the assessments we sent over earlier?"

Colton watched her mind begin to spin, and all the light and easy adventure seeped out of her expression. When he didn't answer, she frowned. "Well?"

He shrugged. "I'm off duty right now. I thought we could find some lost treasure before we start talking shop."

Her small huff made him smile, and he waved her forward. "After you."

"Did anyone bring a . . . ?"

He dug a waterproof flashlight out of his pocket and shined it out in front of her.

"Oh, great. Thanks." She stepped forward into the darkness with only his light shining the way.

"What about bats? Didn't the whole pandemic start because of a bunch of dirty bats?" Omar tried to crouch lower, to shrink smaller into himself, but it was no use, his bulk filled the area around him.

"That was in China. I don't think we have the same problem down here in almost-Antarctica. It's too cold, for one." Ivy wrapped her arms around herself.

"You getting cold? Let's pick up the pace." Colton stepped up beside her. "Wish I could share a sweatshirt or something. But I'm as drenched as you."

"It's all right. I'll be hot enough again out in the sun."

Omar stumbled behind them a little bit. "You okay, dude?"

"Yeah, just fine. I don't like things that fly."

Ivy snorted.

"Except for us. We're the only things that should be flying as far as I'm concerned."

Colton nodded. "That's fair." He laughed to himself, appreciating the things you could learn about your team if you relaxed a little and had some fun.

He walked at Ivy's side for a few quiet moments, and then the cave separated into a fork. "And now. A decision to make." He nodded toward Omar. "It's up to you."

"Let's go right."

"Why, right?" Ivy turned to him. Colton wished he could see what was going on in her mind.

"Because that is the direction of our path."

She nodded. "Makes sense. But what if the treasure is off the normal path; what if it's that way?"

"Does the rule-following, practical Ivy have an adventure-seeking side?"

She lifted her chin. "There is plenty of adventure to be had within the bounds the rules allow."

"And we all know there's no treasure back in these caves." Omar shook his head.

"We do? How do we know that?" Colton egged him on a little bit.

"It would have been found by now." Omar took a step down the path on the right.

Colton looked to Ivy, who shrugged and followed, but when she got close, she whispered, "I say we come back and see what's down the other path."

Her breath, tickling his skin, sent a wave of expectation through him. "You're on."

The smile she sent his way, part conspiratorial, part dare, amped up every bit of interest or curiosity he'd felt for this woman. And he had to stop his hand from reaching out to grab hers. Wow, what was it about her straight, careful beauty that made him want to muss her up a bit? Whatever it was, it had grabbed him, and he was already as entangled in her as he had been with any woman.

Chapter 4

Ivy created some distance between her and Colton. Something about him emanated heat—enticing, handsome heat. And even though her shivering arms wanted a bit of that, she could not in a million years consider acting on any of the new attraction she'd noticed between them. She was pretty sure he felt it too. A complaint letter between them was awkward enough without exploring anything else. Especially when her interest was purely physical at this point, obviously, since she couldn't usually stand the way he handled things in any other part of his life. She amended—the parts that she'd seen, which were entirely work-related. But the way a man flew a jet said a lot about him.

They walked along for a moment, and he surprised her. "Okay. Let's learn some more about each other. Omar, you and Ivy tell me three things you know I don't know about you."

"So, nothing that is in our files?"

"Exactly, or that would come up on a background check.

27

We already know about your brief stint in in-school suspension."

"I was never . . ." Ivy stopped. Colton was watching Omar.

"Shut up, dude. That should have gone away a long time ago."

"Do I want to know?" Ivy asked.

"Just a dumb teacher out to get me. I pushed someone who had it coming."

Colton held up his fist for a bump from Omar. "It was part of the reason we hired you." He looked sideways at Ivy. "If you don't know the story, this guy took on the bully in high school no one else dared to face and punched him in the nose twice and then in the gut before a teacher stopped him."

"I can't believe we are having this conversation. I've punched a few bullies since high school." Omar snorted.

"One of your best qualities." Colton held out his fist for a bump again.

"I had no idea." Ivy looked at Omar with new eyes. "Good for you."

"What?" Colton's wide-eyed, mocking expression made Ivy want to roll her eyes. "Does the rule-following Ivy Hatfield support a little in-school suspension?"

She narrowed her eyes. "I see what you're doing here. And yes. Omar's suspension sounds worth it."

"He was a jerk. He'd just slapped Kirsten's backside."

"Oh, then, yeah. Good for you."

Colton studied her, and Ivy didn't feel like spelling anything out for him; let him puzzle as long as he wanted. Some rules were made to be broken. But not the ones put in place to keep them safe.

"So, what else don't I know about you, Omar?" Ivy stepped up to his side, leaving Colton behind them.

"My favorite color is pink."

Colton snorted.

"No, really, it is. The kind of pink in sunsets."

Ivy nodded.

"And . . ." He stood taller and grinned back over his shoulder at Colton. "I was prom king."

"You were?" Ivy sized him up. "I can see that."

"Whoa, what do you mean, you can see that? You can look at a guy and see if he was prom king?" Colton asked.

"Sure. Look at him. He was a cute high school kid. We know he didn't put up with crap, and . . . yep. I can see it." She turned to him. "You. You were not prom king. But you might have been the class clown."

Omar laughed. "Dude. I can totally see that."

Colton just shook his head. Then he turned to Ivy. "Your turn."

"I think I'll leave high school days behind. Let's see. I win Uno every time."

"You know we're playing that every night now." Omar groaned. "Not the way I imagined my nightlife."

"I'm undefeated."

"That's impossible," Colton challenged.

She shrugged. "Says you."

"Okay, and?"

The intensity with which Colton watched her when he didn't think she noticed made her want to make light of the game, but she humored him and gave him a carrot. "I have a secret wish to own a ranch and ride horses."

Colton stopped walking. In the middle of the cave, his flashlight bobbed.

Ivy and Omar turned. Omar stepped closer. "You okay, dude?"

"Yeah, I'm fine." His smile teased them with a half appearance. "Just . . . stumbled on something." He looked straight ahead, but it was the kind of gaze that was obviously trying really hard to stay that way instead of looking anywhere else.

What on earth had she said? "And for my third, I don't like chocolate."

"What? Now that just ain't right. Who doesn't like chocolate?" Omar shook his head.

"I can't help it. The only chocolate I like is the kind that is pretty much disguised by something else. Chocolate covered cinnamon bears, Snickers bars, that kind of thing."

"Noted." Colton's eyes widened, and his gaze flicked to hers before looking away again. He cleared his throat. "My turn. I was the valedictorian of my . . . *college* class."

"Oh, he's turning it up a notch. At Rutgers? That's a big deal, man." Omar held up a fist,

and they banged knuckles. Again.

"Thank you. *Some* people think I'm a screwup, class clown or something, but no. Turns out, I'm a smart guy after all."

Ivy pressed her lips together. "Most people are judged by their behavior, not their resume."

He dipped his head to her. "And that is a perfect lead-in to my next bit of juicy detail. I almost got kicked out of the Air Force for doing an illegal maneuver."

"Oh yeah. They call it The Fly." Omar high-fived him, and they did some kind of manly dance about it.

"Everyone knows that about you." Ivy crossed her arms, suddenly more irritated than the moment warranted, but she couldn't help it. Why did a perfectly great guy like Colton have to be so reckless?

"What you don't know is that in the same time period I was almost kicked out of the Air Force, they also gave me a medal of honor."

Ivy felt her mouth drop. She hadn't heard that. She didn't think anyone knew that. Everyone talked about The Fly—Flyboy's signature move—all the time. She'd heard about him before she met him. But they didn't know about the medal. "Why don't you ever tell anyone?"

"What?" Colton studied her, his eyes intense in the dark of the cave.

"Why don't you tell people? Everyone knows about the move . . ."

"I didn't tell them about the move either. I'm kind of private guy, believe it or not."

She nodded, slowly, taking in a new side of Colton she hadn't considered before. He was a private guy? One of the most talked-about pilots was a private kind of guy? She wasn't sure she believed him. But she logged that extra information away and kept walking.

"I think I see the end." Omar picked up his pace.

"You not liking the cave, Omar?" Colton stepped up beside him, keeping his feet moving at a faster pace.

Omar mumbled something to Colton, and then Ivy watched a few more moments of Colton making an obvious effort to keep things light with Omar. "Tell me about football. What made you step away from the pros to enlist?"

Omar had been about to play pro football? Ivy didn't know that either.

She stepped closer to hear the response, but it was lost between the two of them. Omar laughed and responded to everything Colton was doing with him. He seemed to feel lighter, and he talked more than Ivy had ever heard him. And before long, they were all standing outside the cave, the sunlight making them shield their eyes and blink a few times.

"Wow, that was amazing." Ivy turned back to see the opening. It was mostly hidden. The entrance faced away from the trail. Even if she studied the patterns on the rock, she couldn't see where one pattern ended and another began. "I would never have known this cave is here."

"But now we do." Colton looked all around them. "Let's mark it, so we remember."

"Good idea." Ivy jumped at the chance, locating a collection of rocks and twigs, and then she and Colton crafted a circle and an arrow on the ground closer to the opening. Her hands brushed his as she laid the last rock. He paused, then reached for her fingers. "Hey, thanks."

She let him cradle her fingers in his for a moment, then she pulled them away. "For what?"

The tingles that ran up her arm were driving her crazy with an insane urge to check out his lips. Were they soft? Firm? Full? She couldn't remember. She didn't think she'd ever looked at his mouth before. But now, it seemed to be the most fascinating thing in the world, judging by her intense curiosity.

She won out and kept her eyes firmly planted, gazing into his, which did other things to her insides. He was so intent, so earnest. She hadn't known Colton to be earnest. And she realized that perhaps Colton had sides to him that she didn't know anything about, sides that might contradict the ones she so intensely disliked.

She stood up, looking away. "I'm not ready for this."

She gasped. Had she spoken out loud?

But when she looked at Colton, he brushed off his hands as if he hadn't heard. She exhaled slowly. But as they made their way back to where Omar waited for them, he said, "I'm not ready for this either." Colton winked and then stepped up to Omar's side again, and the two began chatting as if their conversation were the most important in the world.

Ivy needed to recover. He'd heard. What did he think he'd heard? What wasn't he ready for?

She wanted to stomp her feet in frustration. The unsettled feeling that started to take over her threatened to drive her crazy. Her wet clothes were starting to chafe, and she longed for a hot shower, a long run—anything. Anything to take her mind off of Colton's maddening smile, and . . . what? Interest?

She had no idea. But he was her boss. He was dangerous. He was a goofball, and he had no business running a Top Flight training program; she'd said so herself in a formal letter of complaint. She couldn't forget that. She'd spent all her waking hours of knowing Colton and not liking him . . . She did not like this man, right?

Chapter 5

Colton grinned to himself while he kept Omar talking. He'd had no idea that the tough guy was uncomfortable in tight spaces. But even though Colton was focused on Omar, every part of him was aware of Ivy's motion behind him. Her soft footfalls, her sighs, and huffs. He grinned. So he'd unsettled her. Excellent.

They returned to Fatima's, where the white stucco home with flowers along the front welcomed his tired and wet self as he plodded toward her.

She shook her head. "*Nossa.* You just get inside and in the showers. Those wet clothes can't feel good after the walk you've had. Went in, did you?"

"Yes, we did, but it was lovely." Ivy put her arm around their hostess and Colton appreciated this affectionate side he'd never known about. "What a beautiful spot here, and so close to your home."

Fatima seemed to beam. "Yes, super close. Not many guests brave the water, though." She turned from them to heft what looked like a huge knapsack sheet tied at the top and filled with something. It looked heavy, but she easily lifted it and placed it right on her head. "If you will just head upstairs to wash up, dinner will be ready in about an hour. I know how you Americans like to eat a larger meal in the evening."

"Thank you. But here, let me get that." Colton reached for the sack before she could say anything and placed the whole thing on his own head. It was harder to balance such an unwieldy weight than he thought it would be. "Where would you like me to bring this rather large package?"

Fatima stared with open mouth for a moment, and then she laughed. "You can just follow me." She led the way through the center of the house. "And I won't even mind if you're tracking mud in here."

Colton tried to check his shoes, but then the huge bundle on his head threatened to fall forward.

"Oh, watch it." Ivy rushed forward and adjusted the sheet. "There you go."

"Thanks." He put a hand up to help steady it.

Ivy called out, "If he tracks anything in, I'll take care of it."

"You are the best guests I've ever had."

"Well now, I've always wanted to carry one of these things on my head."

Fatima grinned at him over her shoulder. "What do you think now that you have?"

"I think you have an incredible sense of balance and a very strong neck." Colton followed her out the back door and into a smaller hut.

"You can put that right there in the bin."

The space looked like an outdoor wash hut. There were

lines for hanging with clothespins ready, a large washbasin, and a scrub board.

"Do you do all the washing by hand?"

"I do, but I hire a washing lady to help me. She comes twice a week. It helps feed her family, and it helps keep our sheets clean."

He lowered the bundle into the bin she indicated and then dipped his head. "You have a wonderfully organized establishment, and the others can't stop talking about how pretty it is here. Thank you."

"You leave a good review, then?"

"Of course, and I'll personally recommend you to others."

"*Muito Obrigada.*" Her grin was brilliant, and it lit her whole face.

"In fact, something else I've always wanted to know how to do . . ."

"What's that?"

"Wash my own clothes by hand."

She started to shake her head, but Colton held up a hand. "Would you deprive one of your guests a very particular request?"

"No, I won't. But . . ." She shook her head. "Very well then, come, sit here."

Colton paid close attention while she demonstrated how to use both hands in friction one against the other to rub out every section of the shirt. Then she showed him how it could be swished around in the soapy water, and how to ring out every bit of excess soap before the rinsing process. Then he tried it himself.

Fatima was patient, but he was obviously not nearly as adept as she. By the time they'd washed and rinsed and hung up one shirt to dry, she was probably behind on whatever else she had been planning to do. But she seemed as happy as ever. "And that, my American pilot, is how you wash a shirt."

"Thank you, *Senhora*. I will use this knowledge wisely." He bowed, and she laughed. "Oh, you. Now, go wash up for supper."

When Colton turned to leave, he almost ran into Ivy. "Whoa. Excuse me."

"No, I'm sorry, I'm in your way."

"Been watching long?"

"Oh, well . . ."

"Yes, she's been there the whole time. I think she likes a man with soap on his hands." Fatima winked at them both, and Colton laughed.

"Is it true?"

"What?" Ivy's face was adorably pink.

"Do you like a man with soap on his hands?"

She laughed and turned away. "Generally, yes. I think that is a positive quality."

"Noted." He nodded his head.

She paused on the path, looking up into his face. All kinds of questions lingered there, and Colton didn't want to delve into talking about any of them. Best keep showing her she might be wrong about him before he started trying to win her over into thinking he was right for her. Is that what he wanted? Did he want to . . . date Ivy? He had when he met her. But her obvious dislike of him, her very different approach to life, had almost convinced him that they were completely incompatible.

She walked with him back to the house. "Is it difficult?"

"What?"

"Laundry."

He laughed, a deep, surprised, natural laugh. "Would you like to give it a try?"

"Honestly, yes. And I was so happy you carried that load for her. She looked like she might be swallowed up by the whole of it. How do they carry all that on their heads?"

"I don't know, because it was heavy. And difficult to balance."

"It's incredible. I've always wondered how women carry those heavy loads. I love being here. I love this job. I've been able to go all over the world."

"And fly fast planes."

"Yes, and fly fast planes."

They walked along in such a companionable silence it was hard for him to believe she'd sent such a letter about him. Perhaps he'd already changed her mind? "Fatima said dinner would be ready in less than an hour. And I get the impression she appreciates timely guests."

Ivy laughed. "Noted." Then she turned to him. "Thank you . . . for today. It was nice."

"You're welcome. I appreciate you and Omar coming early so we could do some team bonding."

"It's important. I wouldn't have thought so yesterday, but I think it was a great idea."

He bit his tongue, and instead of teasing her about giving him a chance, he just said, "You're welcome."

Again her face was full of questions. She teetered toward him for a moment, and his heart skipped a little bit with a new, fizzy kind of hope. Nope. This was not happening right now. Not while they were on assignment together, he told himself. But then when her eyes smiled back at him, he wondered if he might just test out the idea a little bit.

"Well, I'll see you at dinner." Her suddenly shy smile warmed him further.

"Looking forward to it."

They headed into their own rooms, which were agonizingly close to each other. How could he keep his focus when he knew she was right next door? He walked out onto the small balcony off of his room, and she exited at the same time beside him, a small railing in between.

"Oh!" She put a hand to her chest.

"Wow, there you are." He shook his head.

"What do you mean, there you are?" She tilted her head, a familiar wariness returning to her expression.

"Nothing . . . You startled me as well. I came out here to think, you know?"

"Well, should I go back in? Give you your space?"

"No, please. It's nothing like that. I'll just go back in. You stay and enjoy." He turned and closed his door. Then he fell onto his bed. This was going to be a long six months.

Chapter 6

The next morning, Ivy awoke unsettled. Her first thoughts were of Colton. Then when she tried to brush those aside, the next thoughts were also of Colton. She groaned and rolled over in her bed. It was lovely and soft, and her view out the window was filled with a patchwork of green trees and blue sky. What would they do today in this enchanting new place?

Since she couldn't get Colton out of her mind, she pulled her laptop over and opened up a web browser. Typing in his name in the search bar felt either sneaky or teenager-ish, but she didn't care. She had to know more about this man. She told herself that principally she was a tiny bit worried that she had misjudged him. But really, she knew that the trickle of intrigue had broadened into an unstoppable river. It wasn't quite the waterfall they had seen yesterday, but she was curious, and she needed to know more.

The first page of search results was all about Top Flight. His missions had been wildly successful, making some part of national news in the various countries. Not quite like her first mission with Ace, which had made international news and created a congressional investigation. She shook her head. Ace was almost as bad as Colton at disregarding typical protocol, but she had nothing but respect for him. He wasn't reckless necessarily. He was smart about things. Was Flyboy the same? A small part of her wanted to believe he was, the other part clung stubbornly to her first assessment of him.

But the next page started to delve deeper into his life. She saw snippets of evidence of his deployments, Afghanistan and Iraq. She saw things she already knew. He was considered the fastest pilot, daring, and an expert with these billion-dollar jets they flew.

Then she saw him with a football helmet at his side, his young eyes sparkling into the camera, and an Air Force football jersey on. She laughed. Ah, so Omar wasn't the only football player. Colton had been a star receiver. A few more clicks and she discovered that he, too, had been drafted by the NFL. But from what she could tell, he never played professional ball.

She dug a little deeper. He was from Texas. The next picture she clicked on took the full screen. Young Colton, maybe high school or early college, smiled at her from atop a horse, a lasso in hand spinning above his head.

So, he rode horses.

She suddenly needed some water. His hotness level just amped up by like a thousand. Something she did not need right now. She pushed off the covers as she pulled up the article associated with the picture. No one knew it, but Ivy had a thing for a guy on a horse. She laughed at herself. She could blame the old westerns she used to read, but really, it was a matter of the cowboy. In her head, they were a dying breed of heroic gentlemen. They lived by a code of good manners and respect for women.

In Ivy's parochial school in Boston, she'd ridden an English hunter jumper for the school's team. And she'd even won a ribbon in an event once, but it had never sated her desire to ride across the plains of the old west. Did such a place exist anymore? She put the laptop aside, her thoughts well and truly distracted by her boss. Her boss. She tried to remind herself that theirs was a business relationship, that she had complained about him just last week, that he did not see her in any way other than a fellow pilot, and that they had work to do.

It didn't matter. Colton up on a horse, after he'd been so . . . new and appealing, was more than her resistance could take at the moment.

A knock at her door made her jump and squeal. She dropped her face into her hands. She had *not* just squealed.

"Ivy?" Colton's voice through the door shot a bolt of electricity through her. She jumped up, ran a tongue over her teeth, pulled her hair back in some kind of bun, wrapped a robe around herself, and opened her door.

"You doing all right in there?" He craned his neck to see past her.

"Of course." She widened the door to show him a perfectly normal room. Then she gasped at her laptop, still open to a full-screen image of Colton on a horse. But he seemed not to notice.

"Yep. Can't see a single reason you should be yelping and hollering in here."

"I'm not. Yelping and hollering. You knocking on my door just surprised me."

"Something you don't want anyone to know about?"

"What? No." She would have given anything at that moment to run to her laptop and close it. Luckily, the screen blackened. She let out a slow breath. "So, what can I do for you?"

"Omar and I want to take out the horses." Did she imagine it, or did his gaze flicker to her computer screen?

Her cheeks warmed. "Do—Do you?" She looked away.

"Yes. But we want to go out early—now—so we have time to go into town this afternoon." He waited, studying her face. When she couldn't find her voice to answer like a normal person, he added, "You in?"

When she nodded, his smile grew. "Okay, then. See you downstairs in ten. Jeans are good. Closed-toed shoes."

She nodded again and then closed the door. Leaning back against its cool surface, she tried to catch her breath. Colton. On a horse. Colton, seeing evidence that she'd been searching him online. Colton. She shook her head. If she wanted to keep any distance at all between them, she must not get up on a horse with Colton.

She closed her eyes. But how could she resist? She loved riding. That land out her window was just begging for someone to tear across it on the back of a beautiful animal. And besides, Omar would be with them. She straightened and hurried to her suitcase. She would go. She would talk to Omar. And she would manage this new, odd fascination with her boss.

But was he really her boss? Ivy was a team leader as well. She'd run several of her own assignments, with the board only remotely involved. They were more partners than boss and employee. Right?

She shook her head, slipping on her favorite soft jeans.

She splashed water on her face, added a touch of mascara, brushed her teeth, and then headed out the door.

Omar and Colton were down on the front porch, and it looked like they were stuffing biscuits in their mouths. Omar waved.

Fatima came toward her. "These boys. They can't even sit at the table to eat their meal." She gestured to a huge selection of fruits and breads and some salami. "Please, eat."

Ivy sat and smiled. "This is lovely. Thank you." She poured herself some juice and filled her plate. "I hear you have horses here?"

"I do. They're really my neighbor's, but we have an agreement. Good animals. Do you ride?"

"I did when I was younger. I loved it."

"Ah, yes. Once you are up on an animal as magnificent as a horse, you don't often forget. It becomes a part of you."

"Yes, it does." She sipped her juice. "This is delicious."

"I make it from the mangoes hanging in that tree out back. We have Aracaju and maracuja also. Coconut water is my base. Maybe you stay longer with us?"

She laughed. "If you keep spoiling us like this, I will be tempted. Everything is just right. Thank you, Fatima."

"And your men." Fatima fanned herself. "Are they as good as they are handsome?" Her grin was kindly, and her eyes twinkled.

Ivy nearly choked on her bit of a buttered roll. "They are good men." She tried to recover her equilibrium. "When they aren't goofing around."

"Ah, yes, men do that. They can't help it. I think they never really grow past the age of twelve."

Ivy laughed. "That would explain some things."

Colton moved past their window, balancing a rock on the

top of his nose. His arms were out, and his head back. Omar laughed and cheered until the rock fell.

"You see?" Fatima wiped her hands on the front of her apron. "But if you can find a good one, they will keep you warm and happy all your days." She moved away. "Enjoy your day."

"Thank you." Ivy considered her words as she savored the last few swallows of her juice. The way Fatima described marriage, who wouldn't want to find someone to keep them warm and happy all their days?

When she exited the front door, both Omar and Colton had rocks balancing on their faces, trying to outdo each other. Omar stood on one foot. "Okay, now switch feet."

"I hope I didn't keep you." Ivy stepped closer.

"No way. I've just got to beat Omar here, and then we can be off." Colton switched feet. The rock wobbled but stayed in place. But then Omar sneezed, and the game was over.

"That just isn't fair."

"All's fair, dude. You should know that." Colton grinned.

As they made their way to the stables at the side of the property, which Ivy now knew sat on their neighbor's land, Omar jogged up ahead. "I want a rematch."

"Any day, man. You're on."

As soon as they were saddled up and Ivy sat on a beautiful speckled mare, she didn't think life could get any better. They had used an English saddle for her, and the other two rode western. Their horses shone in the morning sun. They were healthy, full of energy, and Ivy wanted to prance on the inside with her horse. "We ready?"

"Oh? Does Ivy ride, do you think?" Colton asked.

Omar studied her. "Sure looks like it. Hey guys, don't be letting me fall off this animal."

"What? Omar. You fly fighters. You gonna be worried about a little bit of horse?" Colton clucked, and his horse led the way.

"I'm not worried about it. I just value my back . . . and my backside." He laughed and winked at Ivy.

She snorted.

Colton turned and laughed. "Just trust your horse. These animals know the land."

Omar's horse fell in behind Colton's. Which was good because Ivy was doing everything she could not to notice Colton. They walked out of the main area around the house, and through the first opened fence. From there, land stretched in all directions.

Without warning, Colton shouted. "Hiyah!" And his horse took off out across the pasture.

Omar followed, and Ivy, for a moment, shook her head. They didn't know the land—or the horses—at all. He'd developed no relationship with the powerful, moving force beneath him. One thing she'd learned in her riding was the unpredictable nature of the animals they rode. But no amount of spouting the rules in her mind could diminish her appreciation of the sight of such a beautiful man atop a horse, riding across the pasture.

"What are you waiting for?" Fatima called from the house. "Go taste the freedom!" She laughed and shooed Ivy away with a dishcloth as though she were a young child.

Ivy laughed and nudged her horse. That was all it took for the beautiful mare to tear out after the others. Soon they were in a smooth canter, and she laughed in the wind. She caught up to the others, and the three rode side by side.

The land flew past them in a blur, and Ivy didn't think she'd experienced anything as exhilarating, outside of flying a jet. Colton's eyes were on her, which left a tingling awareness coursing through her. Adrenaline pumping madly, she lifted her hands out to her sides. "Yes!" she hollered, and smiled up into the sun.

Chapter 7

Colton didn't think Ivy had it in her. When she'd stayed behind, he could almost feel her disapproval shooting daggers at his back.

With her hands out, and her face free and smiling, she'd painted such a pretty picture he didn't think he could ever look away.

Who was this woman? Gone was any resemblance to the other Ivy he'd seen. The one who carried around a spreadsheet like it was her Bible. This woman before him looked like there was nothing in the world that would hold her back. The power of her freedom struck him, and he remembered once again why he flew planes in the first place. It was that look right there beaming out of Ivy while she rode horses, that joy. Did she look the same when she flew?

They rode out to the end of the pasture where Fatima had told him there was a patch of green grass and a small stream-fed pond. When they each hopped off their horse, Omar groaned and walked around with a full wide-thighed duck waddle. "I will never be the same. Dude, I'm gonna be sore while trying to train the pilots. Is that what you wanted?"

Colton laughed. "You're gonna be just fine. Look at Ivy. It's like she was born on a horse."

She was rotating her arms in a semi stretch that emphasized the length of her beautiful body, and Colton had to force himself to keep things light. Wow. What a woman. Seeing her on a horse like she was . . . that image was going to stay with him for a long time. Too long.

She turned to Omar. "It's gonna hurt tomorrow. No doubt about it. Not all of us have been riding horses since we could walk."

Colton studied her. Would she realize she'd just given away an intimate knowledge of his past? Seeing his face on her computer screen, an old high school picture of himself, had done things to him, more things than were already racing through him in response to Ivy. She'd googled him. His grin started small. "You maybe haven't ridden for as long as I have, but you're both naturals. You look like you belong on a horse." His eyes watched Ivy, who disappointingly did little in response.

But Omar made a huge fuss. "Well, I'll be sitting over here, holding up this tree, if you need me. If my eyes close, don't even think about messing with me, Flyboy."

Colton looked up into the sun. "Well, I'm going to take a dip."

"What? Again?" Ivy looked like she might turn and run.

"You nervous?" He grinned and then pulled off his shirt, totally gratified with her obvious perusal of his upper half. But he deflected. "The water around here is perfectly safe. Though it might be chilly." He made his way to the edge, but he didn't dive in as he'd planned. He still had his jeans on, and suddenly, he thought stripping down to his compressions would not be the funny idea he'd originally thought. So he just dipped a hand in and showered his top half with water. As the rivulets ran down his torso, he enjoyed the refreshing feel on his skin.

"Now that's just unfair," Ivy said as she approached.

"What?"

"You, stripping down to your skin and splashing water all over yourself."

"It's perfectly fair. You're welcome to do the same."

Omar snorted.

But Ivy stepped closer and raised one eyebrow in challenge. "Just what are you saying, Lieutenant?"

He stood taller, drinking in this bold and daring Ivy-woman he'd never known existed. "I'm saying, you're more than welcome to strip down and get a little refreshing water on your skin." He winked. "Or keep your clothes on, whatever suits you." He wiggled his eyebrows, lightening the moment that was starting to overpower his good sense.

"I just might." She turned from him, ready to pull a shirt off over her head. He swallowed twice and shared a look with Omar, who was deliberately looking away like Colton should have been. But when Ivy tugged at her shirt, lifting it up over her head, she had a tank top underneath.

Colton exhaled, and some of the tension left him. Was it relief or disappointment? Or both? Relief, certainly.

She moved to the water and let some of the coolness drip down her front. He did look away as her shirt became wet through. And for the first time, he wondered if asking for Ivy to be on his team was such a great idea. He'd wanted to win her over, yes, but he hadn't counted on this intense new attraction between them. She felt it too. How were they to work together with this distraction going on? Omar was going to notice too, and how did that look? Maybe he'd call Ace and see if he would swap assignments or something.

Colton shook his head. The guy was in Brazil, finishing up in the Amazon. Ridley had a team, and Amanda . . . maybe he could trade with Amanda. Mustang loved working with Ivy. They could woman it up together, and Colton could move safely across the world. He watched Ivy turn away and stretch her arms above her head, her firm biceps flexing as she did so. Ivy was a powerful woman, no doubt about it, and Colton . . . he wasn't sure what to do about the power she was starting to hold over him.

After a brief rest and ten minutes of cajoling Omar back up onto his horse, they urged their horses forward again. Ivy sprang ahead. "Watch and learn," she called back over her shoulder.

She led the horse to a low-lying fence, and Colton shook his head though no one could see him. She should not be jumping over fences or anything else with a horse she didn't know well. She was being way too reckless, but there was nothing he could do about it. He gritted his teeth, clenching the reins like they would stop her in her tracks and winced as she approached the fence, but she just sailed right over as if it required no effort at all.

He let some of the tension leave, and he rotated his shoulders. "Don't you be doing that," Colton growled at Omar.

"Easy, boss. I have no plans to let this horse leave the ground. I leave that to man-made gadgets only."

When Ivy circled back to them, all smiles, Colton's frown deepened. "You're out of line, Tenderfoot."

She laughed into the air until she glanced back twice and

must have seen his frown because then her eyes narrowed. "And just what was out of line, Flyboy?"

"You, riding an unfamiliar horse over a fence. You could have hurt yourself, and you could have hurt the horse."

"You need to gain a little trust. I know what I'm doing."

"If you knew what you were doing, you wouldn't have attempted such a thing without walking her through it, without knowing her background. Ivy, you could have fallen." He looked away, unreasonably upset. But before he could blow off any more steam somewhere else, he turned back. "I don't want you out here riding like that again."

She sat taller in her saddle. "And just who is going to stop me?" Her eyes flashed at him in a brilliant sort of way that he might have enjoyed if he weren't so flaming mad.

"I just did. And if you want to stay on this team, you better be paying attention."

"You don't own my free time. And coming from you, the most reckless pilot I've ever heard of, this is really rich." She turned her horse, dug in her heels, and tore off across the pasture, back toward the house.

Omar whistled.

"Shut up, dude."

"I didn't say a thing." He started walking back toward the house. "Not saying anything, but boss, you've gotta get a grip on your feelings for that woman."

Colton's eyes shot to Omar's, and then he looked away. "Is it obvious?"

"To her? Obviously not. To everyone else within twenty feet of either of you? Painfully."

Colton's shoulders slumped. "It wasn't even obvious to me until yesterday."

"I was surprised you picked her for your team."

"Yeah, she hates me. I was just trying to convince her to see things a little differently."

"Oh, she feels things, that's for sure, but she doesn't hate you."

"Did you just see that spitfire spewing things at me?"

"Yeah, I saw it." Omar picked up his pace, and Colton wanted to order him around as well. What did he know? The man was about as emotionally in tune as a slice of steak. He flew off the handle at the slightest provocation.

But he caught up to him. "Are you saying you think Ivy has feelings for me?"

"I'm not saying anything. I'm just hoping I make it through these six months with the two of you."

Colton grunted.

They rode the rest of the way back to the house in silence.

When they got there, Ivy was washing down her mare with one of the stable hands. Another came and took their horses and shooed them away back into the house. With one last look at Ivy, who was pointedly ignoring them both, Colton turned. "I'm gonna shower off this ride. Let's go into town."

"You got it, boss."

Colton didn't even bother to correct him that when off duty, he was not the boss, because that would have just made Omar laugh. And Colton was in the mood to punch people who laughed.

Chapter 8

Ivy let Omar and Colton go into town without her. It was time she started behaving like a professional. Colton might have suddenly morphed into a strong, capable, and even charming person, but the few hours she'd spent with him could not erase all the history she knew about him and that she'd seen with her own eyes.

Where did he get off calling her out for riding a horse the way she'd been trained? He didn't know what he was talking about, and the guy who inverted his plane at the speeds he was reported to have flown had no business talking to her at all about reckless behavior. She shook her head. He was widely known as one of the most reckless, non-rule-following, goof-off pilots that had ever flown a jet. She jerked the clothes off the line in the washing hut behind the house.

"Now, now. At least he's handsome." Fatima laughed.

And when Ivy jerked a head in her direction, the woman laughed even harder. "Oh, come now. I love laundry to beat out some nonsense from a man as much as the next woman, but let's go do something more pleasant, you and I. I pay people to take care of this for me." Fatima rested a hand on Ivy's back and led her back up to the house. Ivy tried not to think of her brother, but all this nonsense from Colton was starting to bring back some feelings she thought she'd gotten over years ago, a whole package of emotional stuff she thought she'd dealt with.

WHEN THE MEN came back from whatever they were doing, Fatima served dinner.

Ivy sat opposite Colton, which was annoying because she couldn't avoid looking at him. At last, she did what she'd been doing for years in the military, and she switched into her professional we-have-a-job-to-do mode. "Were you able to contact the owners of the facility we are using?" Her voice sounded clipped even to her own ears.

"No, I figured we'd just show up at the door and bribe our way in." Colton laughed. When Ivy didn't, he cleared his throat. "We start tomorrow. I suppose we can start talking shop if you like. So, we have a hangar, an airstrip, and two planes. We have a classroom and fifteen pilots. And that's it. But I brought the best of Top Flight with me, so I know we can turn these fifteen men and women into the best their country has to offer. We have six months to do it."

Ivy nodded. "So, have you decided the schedule?"

"Yes. Your dockets will be arriving in your email this evening." Colton cleared his throat. "But if you would like to know now . . ." He pulled out his phone from his back pocket. "I've got an opening debriefing meeting with all fifteen. Then we begin classroom experience. Instead of separating out flying time from classroom time, we will pull out two pilots at a time to take their turn in the air. Whoever is not teaching the others will catch the two up on what they missed." He eyed them both. "I have Omar and Ivy on the ground and me in the air for the first two weeks."

Ivy bristled, but she didn't say anything. "What are the classroom hours?"

"We'll start at 0800 until we're finished for the day."

Ivy waited.

"Let's just call it early afternoon. Does that work?" His expression turned stubborn, and Ivy didn't want to push things. "That's great."

They finished their meal in a more subdued tone. When Fatima came in with the dessert, what looked like dulce de leche or caramel flan, Fatima looked around at the quiet room and clucked her tongue, but she just set their plates in front of them and left, mumbling under her breath.

THE REST of the evening continued with Ivy trying to avoid Colton, and him looking at her with a guarded expression. Omar spent the rest of the day joking around with the staff. When the back pasture turned into a soccer field, Ivy slipped on her shoes to join them.

As she approached, the guys called out, but Omar shook his head. "I'd bet Tenderfoot here is a mean football player. Or at least a fierce competitor." He winked at her.

"Does anyone mind if I play?"

The others smiled, most of them goofy, joking expressions, and then she joined Omar's team.

The first time the ball came toward her, and she moved to pass it on, she knew she was playing against men who'd had a ball passing around between their feet since they could walk. They were fast, comfortable, and used tricks she never knew existed. But she laughed with them every time they stole the ball as though she'd passed it right in front of them. They were good-natured about the two Americans who were so obviously outmatched.

Ivy knew the moment Colton stepped out of the door. He came to stand at the side of their game, and her skin tingled with awareness. She cursed that awareness. After watching for a moment, he called out. "Anyone want to try their hand at American football?"

Omar's grin started small and grew. He shrugged. "Maybe. They'll probably whoop us at that too." He kicked at the dirt.

And Ivy almost laughed. What were they up to? "I'm in." She raised a hand. "Wait, are we tackling?"

"Nah, let's just play touch." Colton held up a football. "You guys want to give it a go?"

They divided up teams again, and pretty soon the game became the Omar and Colton show. The cool evening air helped, but everyone was sweating and running hard. Soon all shirts were off, and Ivy's tank top was soaked through. She huddled with the guys. She and Omar were against Colton, but they had some really fast guys on their team. Omar nodded to Rogerio. "You've got this. You go left, fast, hard, all the way to the end. They can't catch you."

"Igiermo can catch me." Rogerio pointed to the other scraggly looking skinny guy on the opposite team.

"I'll take care of Igiermo." Omar cracked his knuckles, and the guys laughed. He put his hand in the center of their huddle. "On three." They chanted. "Win."

Ivy was determined to win. Colton looked too satisfied over there, beating these Brazilians at his own game when he couldn't win at theirs. It bugged her. She told herself it was all about cultural rights, but she knew it was really about beating Colton at something. She bent her knees and watched the ball. It went to Rogerio as planned, but she ran alongside him, off to the side, mostly ignored as Omar blocked Igiermo. Then Colton went for Rogerio. Ivy saw him coming before Rogerio noticed.

"*Aqui*! Over here," she called in Portuguese. Rogerio looked at her in surprise, noticed Colton bearing down on him, and then tossed her the ball.

She snatched it, hugged it to her chest, and ran the rest of the way to the goal line without a problem.

Her team gathered around her and lifted her up on their shoulders. She yelped and steadied herself, laughing.

"Ivy! Ivy! Ivy!" they chanted. All these happy faces looking up into her own lifted some of her irritation. Was it really worth being so mad at Colton? She returned his smile and then held her hands high in the air in a large victory V.

THE NEXT MORNING, they rode together in Fatima's old truck. One of the stable hands drove them. Ivy sat in the back, wedged between the broad shoulders and thick legs of Colton and Omar. She leaned forward for a little wiggle room. At her feet was her work satchel. She concentrated on the clipboard inside, her morning assignments, and the profiles of the pilots they were to work with today.

"I think we need to watch Fernando."

"I agree. I put Omar on him."

Ivy thought that a terrible idea, but she just hummed. Omar was the hot head that Fernando was reported to be. Would they egg each other on? Or butt heads? "I'd like to train the women."

"As part of the larger group." Colton nodded.

"Fine. I think I'll take them to lunch, then." There were five. And from Ivy's experience, it was always better when the women stuck together.

They arrived at the hangar. It was surprisingly clean and new looking, standing out against the charm of the older stone and stucco homes. It sat on the edge of the ocean, the waves crashing wildly onshore in the wind, the deep blue with stark white caps looking more magnificent than inviting.

They parked and walked to the other side, away from the ocean toward what looked to be the door on a nondescript building. Land surrounded the structure, and an airstrip with a control tower marked the place as friendly to planes. Otherwise, Ivy would have thought it an unremarkable warehouse.

The door opened with the code they were given, and they stepped into the building. The sight of two beautiful planes tightened her throat. She always got emotional when seeing the jets she had been trained to fly. She approached and then ran her hand along the side. Out of pure rote habit, she began an inspection of the first plane. She jerked on the parts, poked and prodded from the wheels to the pilot's seat. Completely unaware of anything else around her, her memories raced through her first time in a plane. She relived some of her engagements over Afghanistan. She closed her eyes, breathing in the smell of the fuel, and her fingers itched to take the plane up into the air as high as it would go.

"It never leaves you." Colton's voice, low and rumbly near her ear, didn't startle her as much as it amped up every emotion.

She turned to him, his face close, his body almost intimately placed with one arm leaning on the plane, peering over into the cockpit next to her. "I'm dying to go up in one."

The words came out in a reverent hush. He would never understand just how much she valued even the ability to do so. No one who hadn't ever been barred, or who hadn't gone through some of the emotional baggage she'd had to overcome, would understand.

His eyes filled with understanding, and then his mouth quirked. "Me too."

The look they shared could have made her forget all their past interactions. A sort of understanding, a power between them, settled inside and started wreaking havoc on her determination to remain a professional where he was concerned.

"Hey, Omar," Colton said.

"Yeah, boss."

"We're gonna take up a plane. Hold down the fort until we get back."

"Wait, what? Aren't the pilots arriving soon?"

"Yep. And I know you can handle it. Do our standard introduction. Tenderfoot and I will fill in when we get back."

Ivy's heart hammered inside. Did she dare? Shouldn't she be there to greet the students? Was Colton being irresponsible? A bold twinkle lit his expression, his eyes daring her to resist all claims of responsibility and answer the call to go up in this jet, to fly high and far and with Flyboy. She grinned. "Omar, you'll be just fine."

She ignored his grumbling, and she and Flyboy went to suit up before she could change her mind. "We have to inspect the equipment, right? See if they really fly?" She laughed at her last-ditch effort to give their flight together a responsible purpose.

"We absolutely have to test the equipment. And you're gonna be pilot."

She pulled the helmet over her head. "Me?" Her smile grew.

"Yep, 'cause I'm supposed to do flying checks now and then on all our trainers as well."

Something niggled inside her—a sort of unrest. His comment reminded her of their professional relationship. But she pushed all concerns aside, and she and Colton headed back to the plane. "Then, we're actually following the rules to take a plane up?"

"Mostly." He shrugged and then climbed up into the plane.

When she sat in her seat, the engine roaring beneath her, Flyboy behind, everything seemed to click one step closer to where things should be.

"You ready for this, Tenderfoot?" His eyes smiled at her on the screen from behind.

"You know, I still pinch myself that this is my actual job." Their eyes met. "You do know I love my job, right?"

"Just not always your boss?" His sincerity warmed her. And for a moment, she almost opened up to him.

"My boss is growing on me." Too bold? She held her breath. Perhaps. But she was feeling pretty daring.

"I'm glad to hear it. Now let's get this bird up in the air."

"Now you're talking."

They made their way to the stretch of runway, and then she gunned it. Colton's voice, cheering from behind as they raced up into the air, made her laugh out loud, and soon she was cheering right along with him as they soared up into the sky.

Chapter 9

Colton watched Ivy's face as they burst into the blue. Her face mask was open, her mouth twisted in an almost painful yearning, and her eyes alight. If joy was poignant, Ivy was the poster child for it.

And Colton wasn't far behind. Everything around them was a shade of Colton's favorite color. The smattering of white now and then, the sun rising in the sky, the ocean stretched out on one side, and the beautiful South Brazil coast on the other, everything filled him. But more than that, he liked the smell.

"I love the way these planes smell," Ivy said.

His mouth dropped open, but he didn't tell her she'd just said his exact thoughts.

"Okay, Tenderfoot. Show me what you can do." He grinned behind his mask, intuitively sensing she wouldn't like that challenge. Ivy had a daring edge, a competitive glint that Colton could not resist, but she was governed by the strongest sense of dedication to structure and governance he'd ever seen. It was like the woman raged inside a spreadsheet. And right now, she was probably up there biting her delectable lower lip, trying to figure out just how much to show off and still follow all the rules.

He waited, grinning.

"I can see your smile, you know."

He laughed. "No, you can't." His mask covered half his face.

"It's beaming out of your eyes. I don't know why taunting me is so enjoyable for you . . . but hold on." She pulled back so fast he felt like his whole body was thrown to the back of itself against the seat behind him. The Gs hammered against him, and his skin felt like it might stretch and sag when they were done.

They rode straight up until even Colton wondered if he should say something. Then she shifted again and let them free fall, the tail dropping, the nose twisting, the plane picking up speed from gravity alone. His stomach dropped to his toes. "Wuh!" No time for laughs, he watched their readings.

When she engaged the throttle again, they shot forward, and the momentum felt comforting. She tore across the horizon, finding her way out to the ocean.

They went through all the basic training exercises, and Ivy performed them all with precision.

"Well done, Tenderfoot. It's time to bring her home."

Her soft sigh found a way to his heart where it caressed him for a moment. "It's hard to land."

She turned the craft. "Even though I know I'll go up again, at least I hope so, I'm always sad to quit."

They began to lower in altitude.

"I like the way it smells too."

She lowered the plane the rest of the way in silence. She

was probably mourning the end of the flight, and he was mourning seeing this side of her.

"You're an excellent pilot. I would fly with you any time."

"Thank you."

"But next time we're trading places."

She didn't answer, and he couldn't even begin to guess what she thought about him taking the controls next time. She probably didn't trust him. Then he realized part of her problem with him was trust. In everything. She didn't trust him because he moved outside of her expected boxes.

When they walked in together, Ivy picked up her pace.

"What?"

"We left Omar to handle orientation all by himself." She glanced back over her shoulder like he was a dufus for not remembering.

"I think he can handle it." Colton checked his watch. "It's only been going for twenty minutes. They're in the middle of the welcome video. Or they should be. Watching Ace's face is always so motivating."

Ivy smiled and then fell back into pace beside him. "You're right. I'm sorry. I just . . . I would normally have been here early, have greeted all the pilots. I know their names." Her voice trailed off, and she shrugged. "You do things differently than I do."

"But maybe different isn't always so bad?"

"Maybe." The gaze she flicked in his direction was unsure.

"I would never begrudge time spent up in the air, especially not in exchange for twenty minutes early for class . . . Ivy, these pilots are going to be with us for months."

Her conflicted expression pinged at his heart. She was correct, as well. He knew it. They gave a much more favorable impression if they were on time, all standing together as a team. It just didn't seem like a good enough trade-off to miss that time with Ivy up in the air. The look she'd given him, filled with yearning . . . he couldn't resist. He knew he couldn't. So he'd given in.

If only one day, such a look could be directed at him.

He cleared his throat. Ivy watched him too closely. Could she read his mind? They approached a door, and he placed his hand on the knob. "Like I said, I have to submit quality ratings of your flying. That flight was work too."

She frowned.

"Hey now, what's this?"

"That's all it was to you? Work?" She looked away.

"What do you want from me? Work or play? Because I can usually do both just fine. But you're messing with my usual."

She stepped closer, and he waited. Her eyes were open, expectant. Was she going to touch him, fall into his arms? Apologize? Agree? Disagree?

"Well? Are you gonna go in?" She reached around him and turned his hand on the knob. The door opened, and Omar waved. "We just finished the video. Excellent timing."

Colton stood taller and clipped to the front of the room. "Very good."

They stayed in the classroom all day. The new pilots seemed knowledgeable, and that always helped. Their own country had already trained them well.

Toward the end of the day, they were about to release the pilots. Colton stood at the front of the room again. "Tomorrow, we are going to start taking you up a few at a time for in-flight training. You will learn from Top Flight how to fly with precision." He grinned. "And, we pride ourselves in helping you see how some maneuvers can be utilized in unconventional ways."

"While still following the book," Ivy piped in from the back.

"Ladies and gentlemen, Ivy Hatfield, our book follower."

They laughed, and Ivy frowned.

"Obviously, I'll be the one instructing you on when to toss the book out the window—"

"Surely, we never train them to toss it out. I understand a need to take some risks sometimes, to prevent death, but it's not as though we are recommending a total disregard to the general and internationally accepted rules of safety in these planes." Ivy obviously tried not to frown, but it wasn't working well for her, eyebrows coming together and all.

"We are saying precisely that sometimes the rules must be broken to save lives." He laughed, trying to keep the tone light. "And to have a little fun." He switched off the screen monitor. "You are dismissed. We will see you bright and early at 0800."

Everyone filed out, and when they were gone, Colton called out, "Omar, could you close the door?"

While he waited, he tried to formulate a congenial response. He locked his fingers behind his back in a semi-relaxed stance, but inside he was tense, every string in his body taut.

Omar got the conversation started for him. "You can't be at odds with each other." He crossed his arms. "Well, you can. You can do whatever you want outside of this room. But that little sparring match, that was unprofessional. And you lost the respect of everyone in the room, one way or another."

Ivy's face paled. "But we can't be encouraging pilots to

break the rules. They're new. They're green. Their country won't thank us."

"They will thank us, Ivy. You aren't on the board. You didn't write the mission statement of Top Flight, and you don't know as much as you think you do. Ace, Bear, Mustang, and I hire specific trainers, like you and Omar, pilots who know that sometimes the safest way to fly a plane is to break a few rules." He stared into her face.

"I can see that. I know intuitively there are moments when you do what you have to do, but how many moments of those actually exist in real life? Isn't it better to just fly by the rules?"

He stared at her for long enough that she turned away. "I already know your answer to that question. Look." She gathered her things. "It's one thing for you to fly the way you do. You're dangerous, and I can't do anything about that. But if you encourage other pilots to do the same, now you're risking lives. More lives." She shook her head. "And I'm not comfortable with that."

She made to step away, but Omar held out his hand, resting it on her arm. "Ivy."

She shook her head and stepped out of the room.

Omar turned back to him. "You should tell her."

"About what?"

"About Afghanistan."

"I don't think it will do any good." He slumped down in a chair. "I'd hate to lose Ivy. But I don't know what else to do to show her that good flying is good flying and sometimes just being in control of your plane is the safest way to be, rules or no rules."

"I think she knows. She's just not looking at it that way."

"You should have seen her up there just now. We did a

massive free fall for hundreds of feet, then she pulled up and out of it like it was nothing."

"See, she understands."

Colton wasn't so sure. "Well, she can't contradict me in front of the class."

"That's between the two of you to figure out. You can't make fun of her in front of the class either. We didn't do Top Flight any favors just now. That's all I'm saying. I can't believe I'm saying this stuff. Me."

"You old hothead." Colton made his way to the door. Ivy was waiting outside. "Thanks, Omar. Maybe Ivy and I can have a minute."

"I think I'd rather have Omar here."

"Fine." Colton's frustration grew. He returned to his seat. When Ivy didn't sit as well, he stood. "Should we sit or stand?"

"I'm standing." Her stance was tight and filled with tension.

"Tenderfoot. You interrupted me and contradicted what I said to our students." He waited for her to say something, and when she didn't, he continued. "If you have a problem with something I say, I need you to express it after class when there are no other pilots around to hear you."

"Then those pilots will be left with a misrepresentation of how they should govern themselves."

"I'm going to say this again. I don't know how many more times I'll have to say it, but I hope this will be the last. You're not on the board. We've already made decisions about what kinds of things to teach the pilots. I'm in line with the mission of Top Flight, which by the way, I helped create. And you are out of line."

"But if you continue teaching the way that you do, you'll be filling the world with more pilots who fly like you do."

"And that would be the purpose."

"I have a problem with that."

"Your problem has been noted. A few times now, in fact. It is painfully clear to all of us just what you think of my flying."

"I don't think making light of my addition to the conversation solved anything."

He considered her. "I had two choices: make light, or treat your outbursts as an infraction. Either way, the goal was to discredit you."

She huffed. He could imagine the old cartoon steam coming out of her ears. But she didn't say anything else, which he found interesting.

"Are we finished here?" He made his way back over to the door.

"I have nothing else to say to you that has not already been said."

"Great. Let's go back to Fatima's then."

Omar walked between them, and for once, Colton was grateful for his relative calm. How odd that Omar would be the most levelheaded of the three.

Chapter 10

Colton didn't even look surprised when Ivy showed up the next morning with her letter of resignation in her hand.

He took it from her, glanced it over, and handed it back.

"That's it?"

"That's what?"

"You're gonna let me fly out of here without another word?"

"I don't imagine you'll be flying out of here any time soon."

"I just gave you my resignation."

"That's what I assumed it was. But you also signed a contract. For six months. So, if you want to resign from Top Flight, that's your decision, but if you break your contract for this job, you might have a hard time finding work anywhere else."

"Would you blacklist me?"

"Of course not. But I'm not going to recommend you either, not when you would step away in the middle of a job." His eyes told her he was serious. She couldn't tell if any of this was personal to him. He'd created such a blank mask over his face that she didn't know what he was thinking. But what he said was fair.

"You're right. I'd like to finish this job, of course. I just wasn't sure if you wanted me to." She hated the vulnerability of her comment, but there it was. She was equally irritated with his methods and embarrassed she had interfered, and she wanted to give him an out if he'd prefer she just leave. In truth, she half-hoped he would give her some kind of reaction, some indication that he wanted her to stay.

"I'll be up in the plane all day today," he assured her. "You and Omar will be working together on most of the classroom instruction. I don't imagine you'll see much of me at all."

She told herself that was a good thing. Then she nodded. "Very well."

The pilots started filing into the room, and she was kept busy with them and Omar for the rest of the day.

AFTER TRAINING, they piled back into the truck, Omar and Colton laughing about some of the stunts the other pilots had tried to pull in the air. Ivy just looked out the window, quiet. How had she let things get like this?

Colton applied the brake. "What's this?"

A woman with a basket of fruit sat in the dirt on the side of the road. A few children ran around behind her, playing in the tall grass. Before Ivy could even hop out herself, Colton had lifted the woman from the dirt, and she and the children were climbing into the cab. Colton hefted her basket and placed it in the back.

Three squiggly little boys squirmed and scurried into the

cab next to her. But when they saw her, they became very still and solemn.

"Hello."

Their eyes widened.

"*Oi?*"

They just continued to stare.

Colton jumped back in the front seat. "Where can I take you?" When the woman didn't answer, he said, "*A onde?*"

The stream of Portuguese she responded with didn't help Ivy understand anything more.

But Colton seemed to grasp something of what she was saying. He turned in his seat and showed her his phone map and his translator, and pretty soon they were on their way to the woman's destination, wherever that might be.

He kept up a friendly chatter with her the whole way, which ended up being a significant distance. Would this woman have walked all that way on foot if not for their help?

They turned up a street that led straight up a hill. Soon, they had attracted an audience. People followed the car all the way up the hill along the narrow road between rows of houses. A crowd was growing, getting larger while they went.

"*Aqui.*" The woman pointed. The car slowed in front of a home with a gate. Her boys were scrambling to climb out. They'd already spotted some of the children they knew, apparently. She stepped out so that they could leave.

Colton moved to the back of the truck and lifted her basket and then followed her to the gate.

She rattled it and put in a key, opening it to a tiled-in area on the inside. The house sat on the top of the hill, and as Ivy compared all the other houses, this one was clearly the most well-kept and it was in a prime location. Why was she stuck on the side of the road with her children so far from home?

But as soon as she walked in the door, a shrill voice came from inside, and what sounded like a harsh scolding gave Ivy the answer. A woman stepped out, dressed in fine clothes, calling to the children to get inside. Her face was pointed, her features harsh. But when she saw Colton and Omar, everything relaxed, the lines disappeared, and she smiled. "Welcome to my home. Thank you for bringing home my nanny and my boys."

"You're welcome. They were stranded. I don't know what they would have done if I hadn't happened along."

She clucked. "Angelica is dramatic. She would have been just fine. Buses run along that line all day."

"We were happy to bring her home. I hope that she will be treated well." Colton stepped closer. "I'll check in on her tomorrow. I know others who would like a nanny as good as she is."

Ivy stepped closer. What was Colton doing?

"Oh, we are good to her. We love our Angelica, ask my boys. They can't live without her."

"I'm happy to hear it." Colton nodded. Then he waved up the stairs at the woman herself and her boys. "*Ate logo!*"

She waved in response and then scurried away with the boys in tow.

When they climbed back into the car, Omar grunted. "Do you think she's gonna be good to her?"

"No, but once I send a guy by for a few days running, I bet she'll change her tune."

"You would do that?" Ivy couldn't wrap her head around this other side of Colton. It just didn't seem to mesh with the reckless, careless sort of man she thought him to be.

"Of course." He didn't turn to her. His attention seemed

to have been distracted by something across the way. "Is that what I think it is, Omar?"

She and Omar followed his gaze.

A group of guys playing soccer in an open area of dirt was not usually something to draw much attention, but Colton closed the door. "Let's go check this out, shall we?" He pocketed the car keys and started walking in that direction.

Omar jogged after him, and so Ivy was left to herself, her feet dragging slower the closer she came. It wasn't as if she didn't like soccer—or football, as they called it. She just couldn't figure out Colton. And one thing had begun to tug at her conscience. He obviously had a good heart. What if all her judgments of him had been misplaced? Or at least some of it. Today he had seemed less reckless and more careful. Could a person deliberately choose to set aside the rules? Why would someone do that?

When she arrived at the dirt field, the men were already chatting in the center, Colton with lots of smiles and gestures. At last, after what looked like some haggling, they placed Omar and Colton on opposite sides, and the game restarted.

She sat at the side on the dirt, hugging her legs to her chest. Before too long, a soft, small presence at her side made her smile. A child, a young girl, had come to join her. And then another, and another, until she and the children made for quite an audience. She smiled at them all, waving her hand in a small wave. "*Tudo bem.*" A common greeting she'd noticed that basically meant, *How are you?*

They giggled.

"I'm Ivy."

The kids all said her name one at a time, and then she tried to remember their names. There was Amanda, Gilson,

Roberto, Tiago, and several others, and they were all pronounced differently than she would have thought. They spelled them out in the dirt.

After a moment of quiet, the boys cheered.

Colton raised both hands in the air and ran back to centerfield. Had he just made a goal? She laughed as he tried to high five every guy out there, even if they weren't on his team.

Omar huddled up with his guys.

And she started a cheering section with her group.

"What's his name?" Gilson pointed to Colton.

"Flyboy." She laughed.

Gilson's face lit up, and he held his hands out like an airplane. "Fly . . . boy?"

She nodded. "Yes."

"Flyboy. Flyboy. Flyboy." He started chanting, and the others joined him, pointing. Then a few ran in circles with their arms out as if flying.

Colton started to notice. He ran close to them, with his arms out, and then he winked at Ivy and went back out after the ball.

The kids looked like they'd been recognized by a celebrity. They jumped up and down and cheered. And then for the rest of the game, every time Colton touched the ball, they took up their cheers.

Once, Omar came close. He held out a hand to high five the group as he ran by, but they would have none of it. And they started a new Flyboy chant.

Ivy laughed when Omar shook his head and ran back to the game.

The time went quickly, and soon the guys finished their

game. The kids ran to the center of the field, gathering around Colton.

Soon Gilson was up on Colton's shoulders, and the group was laughing and bouncing in place.

Omar came and sat beside her. "I don't know how he does it."

"Does what?"

"Becomes everyone's best friend. Look at him, even with the kids. When did he become Barney?"

Ivy laughed. Then she grew serious. "Do you think he's reckless? Am I totally off base with this?"

"I just don't know why it bothers you so much." Omar shrugged. "We each bring something to the team. Colton brings his talents. You bring yours."

Ivy considered him. She'd have to think about what he said. "Do you think we're ever getting out of here?"

Colton threw the ball back down in the dirt, and it looked like the kids were now dividing up into teams.

Omar stood. "Oh no, he doesn't. I'm out of here. Fly! Toss me your keys." Omar held his hand up. "We can come back and get him."

Colton shook his head. "I'm coming!" He high-fived a few more of the kids and then ran toward them. His face was alight.

Ivy couldn't look away.

"That was excellent!" He jogged up to them. "How often do a couple of Americans get to play some authentic Brazilian football—streetball?"

"Probably never." Ivy laughed.

"They said we can come back whenever we want. They play every night."

When they climbed back into the car, and for the whole

way back to Fatima's, Ivy's mind was turning over possibilities. Who was Colton, really? Did she owe him an apology?

Even though she was now plagued with a new desire to really get to know this man, he seemed more indifferent than ever.

He parked the old truck and took off inside, calling to Fatima. She and Omar were left to walk in together.

"Give the guy a chance."

Ivy's surprise must have been evident.

He held his hands out. "I'm not talking about anything except as your boss. Whatever other nonsense you guys have going on, that's your business, but if I'm gonna work with you for half the year, I'd rather we all figured out how to mesh. You know?"

"When did you become—?"

"Yeah, I know, Omar, the hothead, giving communication advice. Well, I guess when there's nothing to get all riled up about, I like the peace. Whatever. Just figure it out. Give the guy a break."

She didn't see Colton for the rest of the day. After a walk around the property by herself, she called it an early night. Right before she fell asleep, her last thought was that Omar was right, she needed to give Colton a chance. And probably an apology.

Chapter 11

Colton went to work and came home for the next week and hardly noticed anything else around him. He was flying. He was training. Everything should have been going great, but he couldn't feel the spark his life used to offer him. It was like someone had placed one of those photo editing filters on his life, the dreary grayscale one. He tried to pretend it had something to do with his life, his health, less sleep, but really, the reason was Ivy. One hundred percent Ivy.

She'd taken to smiling at him. Not her normal smile, but this half-lipped, careful smile, and he decided he hated that much more than her spitfire anger.

He'd taken to attempting dumb and reckless stunts or saying crazy things in her presence just to get her riled up. But she just kept making that small smile. And he figured he'd lost her forever.

His phone rang. "Ace."

"Hello to you too, bro."

"What's up?"

"Just checking in. How's it going with Tenderfoot?"

"Why? Has she submitted another complaint?"

"That good, huh?"

He ran a frustrated hand through his hair. "It's . . . nothing. We talked about our differences, and now, nothing. No complaints, just . . . You know? It would be better if she was angry about something."

Ace's low chuckle sounded way too knowledgeable.

"Is the training going well?"

"Oh yeah. We got this."

"You could come home . . ."

The silence on the phone lingered, full of dread on Colton's end; he didn't know what Ace was thinking.

"Do you need me?"

"Well, no, but if you're unhappy . . . if it's functioning without you, I'd like to get our executive board to a place where we can choose to be on the ground in the country we're training if we want, but we don't have to be."

"Yeah, that's a good idea." But what else would Colton do with his life? He loved to train new teams, didn't he? Not lately. Suddenly, his Texas ranch and his horse were looking really good right now. "I'll think about it."

"And, Fly?"

"Yeah."

"Don't let her get under your skin. You're my best friend for a reason, and I wouldn't have even considered doing Top Flight without you. You're a great pilot."

"Hey, no one's gonna change the Fly, you know that."

"Good to hear. Give it some thought about coming home. Omar and Ivy can do this. They practically ran the whole Pacific Alliance assignment by themselves. All I did there was cause trouble for them to clean up."

Colton grinned. "The good kind of trouble."

"Of course."

When they hung up, Colton felt better. And braver.

"TENDERFOOT." He called to her as the class was filing out of the room. "Let's go get some churrasco."

She looked like she was about to drop her clipboard, but that same hesitant smile tugged at her lips, and she nodded. "Okay. I'd like that."

"Omar, you in?"

"Nah." He waved. "You two go without me. I promised Fatima I'd work on the chicken coop."

Colton suspected nothing of the kind had been set up between Omar and Fatima, but he appreciated some time alone with Ivy. Maybe they could get things back to where they should be.

As he held the door open for her, she brushed by, her shirt touching his lightly. A pleasant rumble rushed through him. He wanted to lean towards her, to capture more. They made their way to the truck. Omar waved from one of the other pilot's cars.

They drove through the small town and on to the larger connected city. "I heard that Fogao has a restaurant down here."

"Is that the big one in Brazil?"

"Yes, it's supposed to be the best."

"Mm. I'm starving. This was a good idea."

"And we haven't had our own churrasco yet. Though Fatima has one planned for Saturday. Her own version."

"I just hope she keeps making beans. I didn't even think I liked beans until I ate hers." Ivy smiled out the window.

"I hear she's got *feijoada* coming too, her own special recipe."

"Is that beans?"

"Totally. It's a Brazilian dish, usually made more in the north, but she likes it. I think her family comes from Bahia. That's way north, on the coast."

"How do you know so much about this country?"

"Research." He shrugged.

But her eyes widened. "Research for this assignment?"

"Sure. It really helps if you understand the people you're training, you know? I've been working on my Portuguese too. It's paid off."

"It really has." Her smile changed for a moment, perhaps a glimpse of real appreciation in there.

They drove through the small, one-street town near Fatima's house and on to the larger city nearby. "Soldao should have dancing, clubs, and movie theaters. It's a real city. Maybe after dinner, if things go well . . ." Colton forced his face to stay a mask. *If things go well*, what did he mean by that? It could be taken so many different ways. He'd said it without thinking.

"Dancing would be great. I haven't been in ages."

Ivy seemed more relaxed, natural. Her small smile was still there, but at least she was considering dancing. He got more comfortable in his seat. "Excellent. How are you at the country dances? I hear there's such a thing as a true gaucho cowboy around here."

"They're my favorite. I grew up near Boston, and I used to only go to the clubs on country night or swing."

"You know how to swing dance?" This night was getting better and better.

"I love it. If you do too, we're totally going." She turned

in her seat so she was facing him more. "The more I get to know you, I find . . . surprises."

"Surprises? Good ones or more to dislike about me?"

"Good ones. And for the record, there is nothing I dislike about you as a person. I like everything I've seen. You're fun and engaging, and you make everyone laugh. You're a great person, always helping everyone. People love that stuff."

"People? Not you."

"My comments—that letter." She looked away and frowned. Then she turned back to him. "None of that is related to the type of person you are . . . or anything. And besides. I'm relooking at my previous thoughts."

He nodded slowly. "So I still have a chance to convince you?"

"Convince me?"

"That there is more than one way to go about things?"

That small grin grew. And her eyes showed a bit of life. "If you still want to."

"Oh, I do. Believe me, Tenderfoot. I do." The air between them felt thick with expectation. It hummed with friction. More than anything, he wanted to throw his arm over there, wrap it around her and slide her over right next to him in the truck. But he couldn't be so bold. Not yet. If he played things right, there might be a time.

"So, dancing. Dancing is a time to really let that side of me out. You okay with fun as long as people's lives aren't at stake?"

"Totally." She tapped her fingers. "And I'm not certain of my earlier stance that the things you do put people's lives at risk. I'm rethinking that too."

"Wow, so much rethinking." His thumbs tapped against

the steering wheel. "Should we see what kind of music they play in Brazil?"

"Sure. Okay. I'm not even going to be surprised if you start singing along."

They drove the rest of the way, laughing about the different tunes, the soccer kids, and they even talked work for a few minutes, analyzing the different pilots and their needs. She had excellent insight and suggestions about what they might need to work on in the air with him. By the time they arrived at Folgao, she was laughing through her tears, and he was itching to reach over and take her hand.

When he parked, he winked. "You sit tight, because I'm coming around to get your door."

Then he hopped out, feeling like he was on a really great first date.

She climbed down, stepping right in front of him, in the intimate space people usually reserved for those they wanted to get closer to. He grinned down into her face. "And now we are going to have the best meat this world has to offer."

She laughed. "Good thing I like meat."

"If you want, they also have the best salad bar Brazil has to offer. I hardly touch that stuff; it doesn't leave room for the meat."

She entered with a hand on his arm. Dressed in their work clothes, she looked military. He didn't know how else to describe it. Plain clothes, straight skirt, practical. He wore a white t-shirt, stretched across his chest. It fit best under the flight suit.

But she pulled at her hair, and soon it was falling down around her shoulders in waves.

"You know, you have fantastic hair." He itched to touch it, to let the silky strands fall through his fingers.

"Thank you." Her smile grew even bigger. "I'm regretting my outfit, but everyone here seems to be wearing whatever they want."

The restaurant was only about half full, and she was right. Some were overly fancy, and others were even more casual than he was.

"You look beautiful." He didn't watch to see her reaction. He just sent his compliment out there. He would have told any girl if she was beautiful. He felt like there wasn't a woman alive who wasn't. But when he told Ivy, he meant the very specific kind of beautiful that quickened his blood and made him want to pull her closer to his side, the kind of beautiful that simmered from the inside out.

"Thank you." Her small-sounding response drew his attention back to her face. Her eyes were lifted to his and glistened a little.

"I'm sorry for misunderstanding you."

"Hey now, I thought we talked about this. I've got another chance to prove myself."

"But you shouldn't have to prove yourself." She shook her head. "But never mind me. Let's eat."

The maître d' showed them to their table.

They were given a card at their right. On one side was a green dot, on the other side a red dot. "If you want more, just leave it at green."

Ivy flipped the green side up. "It's all green, baby." She stood. "But I'm also going to fill my plate with whatever goodness is over there."

The center of the room was filled with a huge table overflowing with all kinds of Brazilian dishes. From where he sat, Colton could see they had a huge vat of *feijoada*, vinaigrette with tomatoes and cucumbers, hearts of palm, three-layer gelatin, a delicious looking stroganoff, and various fish dishes. Wow. A whole meal in itself sat over there. He'd have to come back and bring all the other pilots. This place was amazing.

The servers wore white shirts and black pants and small black bowties.

Ivy returned after they'd placed the first three rounds on her plate. He laughed at her widened stare at the pile of meats.

"What is all this now?"

He pointed to the small bite-sized piece. "That is a chicken heart."

She nearly choked.

"And that is a piece of an alligator." He laughed. "Everything else you would find in a steak restaurant at home."

"Good to know, and did you eat the heart or the alligator?"

"I did. I love those little hearts. Alligator though . . ." He grimaced. "This one tasted like old fish."

She shook her head. "Nope. No need for me to enjoy that piece then."

"But the gator I've had down in Louisiana . . .Mmm. That's good stuff."

"Where haven't you been?"

He considered her question. "Not many places, honestly. I'm looking at Mount Rushmore as probably the last place standing that I have not explored. The last place of note. I also haven't been on the plains of Kansas, but . . ."

"Well, now, let's not underestimate the plains of Kansas."

He eyed her. "I thought you were from Boston."

"Oh, I am, but I have driven through Kansas, and I'm telling you. That long stretch of the same view is not to be underestimated. I am convinced there is extra land there than the maps lead us to believe."

He laughed. "I can well imagine. Texas is like that. It just keeps on going. When you enter one end, the signs will tell you how many miles to El Paso, which is down south. It's well over one thousand miles."

"Across one state?"

"Yep."

They enjoyed their meal until Ivy looked almost finished. Colton could have eaten another cow, but he was determined to make this night about Ivy. And he didn't want a too-full stomach. Ever since he'd considered holding her in his arms on the dance floor, a stop by the local club had become his number one objective for the night. Did the woman drive him crazy a little bit with her clipboard and her strict under-standing of protocol and rules? Yes. Of course. But the more he spent time with her, when she had her hair down, so to speak, the more he thought he might be feeling the good kind of crazy.

Once he'd taken care of the bill and Ivy had compli-mented everyone on the great service and food, they made their way out to the car. He tried to keep his voice casual. "So, is that club still calling your name?" He glanced at her as nonchalantly as he could.

"Is it calling yours?" Her eyes were wide, hopeful.

So he took the plunge. "Ivy, I've been thinking of nothing else all night. We've got to go dancing. You game?"

"I'm so game."

"Oh, this is awesome." He held out his hand, she took it, and they both ran to the car.

He blared the music on the way over there. When they pulled in, the whole place seemed to be shaking with the sound of music inside. Good, Texas-sounding country. He grinned. "Now this is what I like to see."

"You ready to show these folks what a real Texan looks like?"

"Yes, ma'am, I am. Hold tight." He hopped out, ran around the car, and opened her door.

When they opened the front door, the place was not as packed as Colton feared. The music was just right. They were playing *The Git Up*, and the whole room was involved in a line dance like he'd never seen. "Wow, this place is legit."

Ivy stepped closer. "I love this." Her feet moved. The energy pouring off of her seeped into him. They found a table, she left her shirt on the bench, and Colton found himself with a tank-topped beauty dragging him out to the dance floor like he was in college again. Life just didn't get any better than this.

Chapter 12

Ivy's whole body hummed. They'd gone through five line dances, the music just right, the company amazing. She felt like she'd just become best friends with a room full of strangers. Brazilians had a gift, honestly. They were the warmest, friendliest people she'd ever met. And her date . . . Was he her date? He was certainly acting like it. Had this gone beyond professional relations to something more? She found herself hoping so. Without thinking about it much, they'd been standing closer, dancing closer, and now, as the music slowed, she practically ran into his arms. About time.

As his strong, lean arms held her close, she melted even closer. He cradled one hand in his own and held his other large palm against the small of her back. "Now that I've got the most beautiful woman in the room right where I want her, this night might just have to go on a little longer than it's used to." His grin was warm, relaxed, his eyes sincere.

She tilted her head back and laughed. "I needed this. I really needed this night. I don't care if it lasts forever."

He twirled her around. "What's this I hear about you knowing how to swing dance?"

"Dance competition team in college."

"Really, now this is just about to get interesting. And country dance?"

"That too."

"Leaps? Throws?"

"If you can throw me, I can do it."

"Oh, I can throw you." His eyes sparkled with challenge. She bit her lip. "Then what are we waiting for?"

He two-stepped to the side.

She followed.

He cupped their hands together and then spun her around.

The music picked up with the next song, and they started moving faster to the beat. He started easy. They rotated in circles, stepping from side to side, together and then back. Then he grabbed her by the waist and lifted her into the air.

She grinned, landing at his front.

"You ready?"

"With you? I'm always ready."

His answering grin was too good a look on him. Why was this man her boss? Wow, her feelings for him were as polar opposite as they came. Like a yo-yo, she went from adoring him to hating his methods, to respecting him to wanting to keep her distance, back to hoping for any sliver of attention. She was a mess. But she loved her mess. And she laughed as his thick palms grabbed her at the waist, this time bouncing her on each hip, tossing her high into the air, down along the ground between his legs and then back up front.

Colton held her close for a moment, stepping side to side.

"You know. I knew I would be into you, Ivy Hatfield. But this is a whole new level entirely."

When her eyes found his, the sincerity that shone back reached her. She felt it deep inside. What made Colton tick? For the first time, she wondered why he flew the way he did. "You know, what you did in Afghanistan was incredibly brave."

"You heard about that?" He studied her for a moment. "Not reckless?"

She shook her head. "No. I think it was a calculated risk, and you took it, and it worked."

He spun her again. Then, bent forward linking their elbows, she rolled over his back, landing on his other side.

But he never responded. And she decided it didn't matter. He was a hero. Her country and her military had recognized him. He'd saved lives, more than she ever had, doing what she had labeled as reckless. As she spun once, he spun her again, and again and she felt the tug in her stomach. But as he spun her again, she let go and tipped her head back and cheered. The world rotated, and she laughed.

And she wondered if that was what it felt like just to let go. Then Colton pulled her close, and as she closed her eyes and waited for the world to steady itself around them, she draped her arms over his shoulders and peeked. "You're still spinning."

"Awesome." He held her closer. Then his husky whisper in her ear and the pulse that ran through her at his lips being that close to her skin, thrilled her to her toes. "I've got you."

At last, the world stopped. When she opened her eyes and was caught immediately by an intense look from him, she could only say, "I know."

When they at last began to make their way back to Fatima's, the early hours of morning had crept in on them. Ivy sighed. "Should I feel like I have to sneak in?"

Colton reached for her hand. Then he tugged a little. "You know. You're too far away over there." He tugged again.

"What? You want me to slide closer?" She undid her seatbelt and scooted as close as she could.

"Hey, now. You still have to be buckled." He grinned. They stopped at a light, so he reached across and found the buckle. Then he tightened it at her lap. "There you go. Safe and sound." His kiss on the top of her head was probably meant to be friendly, but that simple contact sent a wave of yearning.

Wow, she was tired. She told herself not to look up. *Don't look up. Don't look up.* But her eyes disobeyed in a traitorous display of feminine desire. He was close. His kissable mouth looked soft but firm at the same time, and close. Everything was close. The very air filled with an intoxicating aroma of his soap—earthy, tinged with a hint of something male. He shifted his body so that he faced her more fully. The light must have turned green, but they were the only people on the road. He reached out as if to run fingers down her face, but he hesitated and dropped his again, landing on her knee, resting there, not moving, but full of expectation. "Thank you. For an awesome night."

"You're welcome. I needed that."

"I hope we're . . . are we good?" The hope, the insecurity, warmed her and sent her heart to him. His gaze traveled over her face and stopped on her mouth. For a moment, she thought he might tip his head and capture her lips, but he stared back up into her eyes in a comfortable caring expression.

She enjoyed the silken moment. Their closeness felt more

intimate than anything she'd experienced. She wanted things right between them. She wanted to break down the barriers she'd created. He didn't deserve her censure, and the arrogance of someone like herself thinking to correct him was much more than she wanted to see in herself. "You're an excellent pilot, Colton. I respect that. I'm sorry for . . . everything."

"No apologies. Not necessary." He rested a hand at the side of her face for a moment then turned to face the front.

The air felt cooler in the space between them, but he reached an arm around her so it rested behind her.

She snuggled closer, wanting to linger in the moment as long as possible. What would happen tomorrow? If she went to bed tonight, and let the evening close, would everything they'd created and experienced tonight end?

Colton parked the truck in its spot along the side of the house. "Stay put."

She smiled and scooted over closer to the other side of the truck. When he opened her door and peered in at her, her mouth turned up at the corner. He held out his hand. She moved to the door and reached for his hand and slid out, but he didn't move away, so she stood in front of him, close enough to kiss. And she didn't know if it was the lateness of the hour, or the incredible night they'd had, or the fact that she hadn't dated anyone in a long time, but she suddenly didn't care one bit about how awkward things might be the next day; she wanted Colton to kiss her. She reached her hands up his chest until they rested almost at his neck. Without even thinking, she stepped in as close as she could.

His arms wrapped around her, sending a smattering of shivers through her, happy tingles.

She stood up on her toes. She could almost reach him.

His grip tightened as his fingers dug more into her back, his body going tense, his eyes dark. She thrilled with expectation. *Kiss me.* As she stared into his eyes, she saw the hesitation, and she wanted to kiss it away, to kiss away every thought that told him to wait. Colton's recklessness seemed to course through her. What would he do? Live in the moment, take a chance, go after what he wanted? She wanted him. *Do it, Colton.* Her mouth went dry. She licked her lips and waited.

He leaned in as if his body was swaying, rocking, desiring her, resisting her until she thought she would go mad with her own desire. With one last rock forward, he pressed his lips to her forehead again.

She leaned into him, leaving no doubt as to her wishes. And when he stepped away, she swayed in place, placing a hand on her stomach.

"Let's get you into bed."

Her eyes widened, and she placed a hand on her mouth.

His face darkened, turning a dark red. "In your room." He placed a hand on his forehead. "I didn't mean that the way it sounded." His eyes held an apology. And for a moment, she let him wallow in his awkwardness. Then she laughed. "Let's get me into bed?"

"Yeah. Um. By yourself. Tonight . . ." He turned away. "Could this conversation get any more . . . ?" He eyed her again.

She started to shake with the effort to laugh quietly. She had to laugh or else consider such a thing, which would be disastrous. Both for her personal morals and for the complete lack of ethics for an employer-employee relationship. And she valued her job at Top Flight. How would that be to create problems with Colton, one of the executive board members?

She just couldn't go there, but a kiss? She sighed. Now that was not going to happen.

Colton turned toward the house, her fingers laced with his, and they tried to move as quietly as possible through the front door and up the stairs down the hall, until they stood at her door. She turned to face him, but he just lifted the back of her hand to his lips, sending a new round of shivers through her, and kept walking to the next door. He stepped inside without another look in her direction.

Once inside her room, she shut the door behind her, leaned her back against it, and closed her eyes. As her breaths left her one at a time, she tried to calm her body and prepare to rest, hoping to sleep the remaining four hours of her night. Knowing she would never find rest if she didn't relax, she stepped into her bathroom and turned on the shower.

Chapter 13

Colton arrived at the hangar early the next morning. He'd grabbed one of the bikes on the property and rode in, leaving the truck for Omar and Ivy.

He needed to go through some of the paperwork. Amanda had been asking about some things. But he could do paperwork anytime. The real reason he had left so early was perhaps cowardly, perhaps gentlemanly. He wanted to give Ivy her space in case she regretted every moment of her asking to be kissed. She hadn't said as much, but she'd put herself out there, and it had taken every bit of self-control in Colton's arsenal to resist.

How many times had he argued that whatever they did would be fine? They could weather it in the morning. It was late. But those were not reasons to kiss a woman, no matter how irresistible she became, no matter how much fun they'd had, no matter how much he wanted to earn her good opinion, convince her to like him, wipe away her doubts. Kissing her would not be the best move, and the tiniest rational part of his brain had carried through every other desire pounding with deafening beats through the blood at his ears.

And now, he wanted to give them space this morning to work through whatever they were feeling, to help her if she regretted every second of their evening.

He shut down his laptop when the last file was sent to the group drive for Top Flight. He sat back in his chair, looking out over the rough ocean. The winds had picked up; the white caps of the dark-blue waves extended farther out into the ocean. But the sky was clear of clouds. It would be another great day for flying. The team was progressing. They were excellent pilots already and would become more so.

Colton was proud of Top Flight, of the program they'd developed. He was proud of his team. Ace, Bear, Mustang, and himself had really put together something epic. He'd joined for the money. He'd told them flat out, "I'm here for the money." But it had turned into much more than that. And he now considered the work they did as important.

"There you are." Ivy's voice amped up his awareness on all levels.

He turned, pasting a smile on his face, belying the nervous pounding in his heart. But her smile was large and warm and unassuming. Omar stepped in behind her. She clipped across the room, clipboard in hand. What used to annoy him, he now found endearing. "Omar and I have been going over the pilots in preparation for their reviews. And we wanted to get your opinion on a few of these."

"Oh, excellent." He sat at the table, and the other two joined him. Things seemed normal between him and Ivy. So normal, he didn't know what to think. She hadn't even given him anything extra to go off of, no smile, no double look, nothing intimate, nothing uncomfortable. Not even anything awkward. He admitted to himself that he was disappointed. But he was not deterred. They went over each of the pilots and filled out the paperwork to use in their reviews.

"I can start pulling them from class and doing personal interviews." Ivy looked from Colton to Omar. "Unless you think we each need to be there."

Omar shook his head.

Colton nodded. "That's great. I'll do their exit interviews. You're the best one to do this initial assessment. Omar can talk to them at the midpoint."

They discussed a few of the other details, some of the issues they'd been having, and then closed up the meeting just as the first pilots began to arrive.

Before Colton slipped out the door, he pulled Ivy aside. She still looked perfectly professional and undisturbed. He stepped closer. Still no response. He wanted to place a finger at her wrist and check to see if her heart rate was thumping through her like his was. "So. Some of the guys were talking, and they said that Padre Chagas had a fun nightlife. It's full of restaurants and bars and lined with flowers. There's a park in the middle."

"Oh? That sounds fun. We planning some after-work team bonding with them?"

With them. "Yes. Excellent idea. I was thinking of bringing it up today during our wrap up."

"Great. I'm in." She smiled. Not the tremulous, apologetic smile, not the full we're-dancing-together smile, just this impartial professional smile, and Colton wanted more than anything to break through that new ice. "Come with me."

He turned to walk out the door.

"Wait, what?" Ivy looked back at the pilots who were all

seated and ready. Omar raised his eyebrows from the front of the room.

"It will only take a moment." Colton held the door open.

She followed him out. He wasn't sure she would. And now that she had, he wasn't sure what he was going to do. But he led her around the corner from the classroom to an empty hallway. Then he turned back. "Saturday."

"Hmm?"

"Saturday. I want to take you out. On a date. Again."

The pleasure that flashed through her eyes could not be hidden, and it emboldened him. She looked away, battling something. He could only guess at what. Then she said, "Okay."

"Great. Be ready at noon." He grinned, then stepped away. "And I'll take you with me tonight. No need to hop in a car with any of these others."

"Got it."

He turned and walked back past the classroom and out into the hangar. He'd be up flying the rest of the day, but already, he was counting on some fun with Ivy tonight and tomorrow. He rotated his shoulders. She hadn't quite melted at his feet or blushed in embarrassment, but she'd said yes. Tomorrow would be epic. He'd make some calls tonight, call in some favors.

HOURS LATER, they were finally all back in his truck. He had thrown his bike in the back, and they were on their way to Padre Chagas. Omar's feet were tapping. "You know, these pilots. They're cool people."

"They are," Ivy agreed. "I'm glad Flyboy thought of this. It's fun to get to know them better."

Colton thought it incredibly ironic that she would say so, but he nodded. "Team building, right? We are supposed to have an activity with them once a month, right?"

"They all usually go to a pool hall together. I might start joining them." Omar didn't look at Colton. But his tone was the kind of pretend casual that Colton almost called him out on, but Ivy shook her head, and Colton caught the motion in his rearview mirror. Interesting.

"Cool. We've been using this truck, but if we need to go back and get that rental, we can do that too."

"I'll think about it. The guys have a car, and there just seems to be less of a need for one here, you know?"

Colton nodded. "The bike ride this morning was great." He pulled up to an overly crowded lot. "This place is on fire." Energetic people filed onto the street from their cars. Music blared from somewhere partway down the street, and strings of lights lit the night sky. He was about to say, "Hold tight," so he could get Ivy's door, but she jumped out before he could. He rotated his neck.

Omar laughed. But he got out of the car before Colton could ask what was so funny. The pilots all stood in a group, waiting for their threesome. They had a few women, but mostly men. Ivy went to stand with the women, and everyone seemed pleased. "Okay, should we see how the gauchos have fun?"

"*Isso!*" One of them gave him a high five. "*Vamos.*"

They stopped into a restaurant for dinner. It was delicious. Then Omar waved his hand down the street. "How about a drink from each bar!"

They laughed. Colton had never seen so many bars in one place. He was tugged into the nearest one while Ivy waved. The girls started dancing in place. Was she going dancing? He craned his neck but couldn't see where they had become lost in the crowd.

The guys ordered their first of many rounds. Colton spent the rest of the night hoping to be closer to Ivy. They never caught up. She didn't drink, unlike Omar, who was starting to slur his words. Colton didn't either, but he felt responsible for the group and knew work would come early tomorrow. Every time he looked Ivy's way, she was the only one without a cup in her hand. Interesting. Something else he loved about the impeccable Ivy Hatfield. Now that he'd seen her unwind, now that he'd taken her dancing and up in the air, he knew there was more to her orderly discipline. She was a real emotional whirl with fire in her veins. He liked that not many knew that about her.

But no matter how much he wanted tonight to be about them, he never did get to spend time with her. The other guys were tight with Omar.

"Sing! Sing! Sing!" A whole group of them surrounded him.

Colton laughed. "What?"

And then Omar started singing in Portuguese, swinging his cup around. Colton stepped closer. Ivy stood beside him. "That's the Brazilian national anthem."

"Is it?" He laughed. "How does he know that?"

She shrugged, laughing. "Maybe you're not the only one who does their research."

"Apparently not."

The other pilots egged him on, and Omar kept going until the very end. They all held their cups up in the air and then downed the rest of their drinks.

"I wonder if Omar is part Brazilian." Colton sidestepped so that their arms touched, just barely.

Ivy didn't step away.

"You're not drinking."

She lifted her eyes to his face. "Neither are you."

He nodded. "Does that mean you're taking the truck, and I'm driving all these rabble-rousers home?"

"Or we put them all in the back of the truck, and I drive in the cab with you and maybe Omar . . ." They both turned. Omar was threatening to stand on the table for his next rendition.

Colton laughed. "I love that guy."

"You gotta love Omar."

When they were all finally ready to call it a night, Colton was pleased that a good bunch of them had made arrangements and were getting rides. He helped the rest of them into the back of his truck, including Omar, who thought it would be more fun back there. And then Ivy pulled up addresses and the map function on her phone and headed toward the first home.

Within about ten minutes, the guys who were in the back seat were cleared out and home. Things were pretty quiet between the two of them. Colton studied her in between watching the road. "Talk to me. Where do you see yourself after Top Flight?"

She turned in her seat so she was facing him from the passenger side. "Who's asking? My boss, or . . . ?"

"Not your boss." What was he? He wasn't going to spell anything out right now. The man who wanted to kiss her? The guy who was more intrigued by her than he had ever been by any other woman?

She fiddled with her phone. "I don't know."

He watched her for a second then turned back to the

road. "You seem more concerned about the answer to this question than I would have thought."

She waited so long to respond that he wasn't sure she would. Then the quiet voice that began was so different from all the different sides of Ivy, he almost pulled over so that he could really pay attention.

"I don't know if you were the same, but when I was honorably discharged from the military, I felt a little lost."

He didn't respond. He'd been a mixed bag at his discharge. Lost without a plane to fly, but kind of ecstatic that no one was telling him what to do all the time.

"I tried everything I knew to do. I finished my degree. I worked for an accounting firm. I even tried sailing."

He laughed. "Sailing?" Things were looking even better than he imagined for his plans tomorrow.

"Yeah, it's a thing around the Cape. I loved it. But it can't be my way to earn a living, you know?"

He nodded.

"Top Flight gave me purpose again. While you resist the structure and the rules, I need them. I feel comfortable a bit boxed in."

Now that was something he couldn't even imagine understanding as long as he breathed. But he respected that she felt that way.

"So, you might work for Top Flight forever?" He considered such a thing. He'd never said anything that committed in his life. He preferred the open method of viewing his plans.

"Won't you?"

He shifted. "I imagine I will. Unless something else comes up—unless something happens. I don't know. Can we ever be certain about anything?"

"I guess not. But you do think it will be around for a while . . . don't you?"

"Oh yeah. We're not going anywhere. We have plans to grow. Other skills in the military, everything. We've got some homeland security guys in mind. They can hire out as consultants on any number of security issues."

She nodded, seeming pleased.

They dropped off the last couple guys from the back of the truck, and then once back at Fatima's, Omar stumbled out and made his way into the house.

"He's going to feel that in the morning." Colton turned off the car. He put his hand on the door handle, but Ivy stayed where she was. So he turned back.

"I'm not really ready to go to bed yet."

Colton craned his neck to the sky. "The moon is out. Should we go for a walk?"

"Yes, thank you. If you're not tired. I need to walk off my thoughts."

They headed for the path at the edge of the woods on the side of the house. "I think there's a coconut grove up ahead and a bit of a garden next to it."

"The Aqua de Coco we drink in the morning? Is that from her own coconuts? It's the sweetest I've ever had."

"Yes, Fatima told me it was. If you show up at the kitchen early, you can eat some of the clear flesh of the coconut right after they cut it open."

"Oh, this secret you have kept all this time!" She swatted him.

"Maybe we could sneak in there and cut one for ourselves."

"Oh, no. Let's wait for morning. I don't want to upset what Fatima has already planned for tomorrow."

"If we find one ourselves in the grove . . . then it won't be upsetting anything."

"True." She smiled, and with the moonlight shining down into her eyes, and her face lit with the silver glow, he wished to see her just that way forever.

Chapter 14

The lateness of the hour descended on Ivy like a warm blanket. And she felt . . . at ease. Colton walked beside her. "You know. I've not seen such excellent flying as you showed that one time we were up together," he said.

"Oh?" Pleasure rippled through her. "Thank you."

"I'd like to do it again."

Technically they didn't have any need to go back up together. But she couldn't deny how tempting the offer was. "Maybe we can go up again in a month or so? We could do the first day of dogfight training together," he continued.

She smiled, enjoying the thought. "Do you think anyone could possibly catch us yet?"

"There are a few. Honestly. We're gonna have to be on our toes if we want to make sure they don't win a fight too early."

"Got some arrogance going on up there? I could think of a few that might need to be taken down a peg."

"Especially by you. I'd like you to make it as quick a shut down as possible."

She laughed. "And destroy their fragile egos?"

"I don't think there's any danger in that. No. But I want them to see how quickly things can get hairy in a life or death situation."

She nodded, knowing she was only hesitating for show. She would jump on this chance. "Awesome. When do we go up?"

His grin spread across his face. "You know, we could just take the plane up for a follow-up look at your flying . . ." The hopeful fun in his face, the moonlight, the lateness of the hour, all of it combined to make her feel like stepping closer was the most natural thing in the world.

"I don't know if that's such a good idea, Lieutenant."

He moved around to her front. "And why's that? The plane is available. I'm here. You're here."

She looked up into his face, his jawline sharp against the moonlit shadows. His eyes warm, his mouth . . . She swallowed. She wanted this. He was nothing like her old co-pilot Guido, or her brother. He was strong, brave, expert. His moves were more advanced. Reckless? Possibly.

His hands reached out to pull her closer. He stepped into her intimate space, running his hands down her back, sending shivers of expectation through her. She couldn't look up, not yet. But he pulled her close, hugging her like she was precious to him, with gentle pressure. Then a kiss at the top of her head and she was done waiting around, done second-guessing, finished pausing in the shadows of her desire. She liked this guy. And who cared if he was reckless? Maybe that's what she liked about him. What had changed besides a sudden and insane desire to kiss him?

His eyes sparkled at her as he moved ever closer, his mouth leaning closer to hers.

Her trust. She trusted him. Her feet went up on tiptoes. She stretched her arms up to his shoulders, her hands went to the back of his neck, her fingers rising up into his hair. It felt soft; the short, military cut on the back tickling her skin.

As his arms circled around her more completely, and the bubble of safe trust turned to a delicious, tickling sort of hum, his mouth found hers. The hunger that surged surprised her, but she embraced it. She responded with the power of her desire, wiping away his hesitance. His grip on her tightened, and his kisses became more urgent.

She bit into his upper lip, trying to get more from him than a kiss would allow. The slight scruff on his chin and mouth felt delicious. She arced against him, and his fingers spread against her waist, spanning the small of her back. He dipped her, capturing her better at this angle. Her fingers went up into his hair, grabbing fistfuls and everywhere, coursing up and down her core, paths of energy surged, hot and intense.

Then his kiss softened and slowed, and tenderly, he pressed his mouth against hers, again and again, enveloping her in a tenderness that took over the urgency and turned it into an overwhelming fire. And then he stopped, kissing her nose, her cheek, her chin, until she opened her eyes. "I could do this all night, except that unless you want to lay down in the dirt, we've got to take this inside."

She laughed, leaning her forehead against his chest. She shook her head. "Let's go to bed."

"Hey, now, I wasn't saying we should end this night."

His face was earnest, intent, tender still.

"What are we doing in a few hours for our date?" She grinned.

"Oh, now don't you try to ruin your surprise, little lady. You'll just have to wait and see."

"Until tomorrow, then?" Her breathless whisper filled the air between them with promise.

"Tomorrow is just getting better and better." He reached for her hand, and they walked back to the front door together.

He kissed her again at her door, the kind of intimate kiss that said, "We do this now. Your lips are part of my familiar space." And she melted into him.

"Goodnight." She whispered to him and then closed her bedroom door, trying to pretend he wasn't sleeping on the other side of a thin wall.

THE NEXT MORNING, they sat together at breakfast. He didn't hold her hand, but they were close enough their shoulders brushed. Omar was nowhere to be seen. Fatima's cheerful smile and the delicious food made for a near-perfect morning. Colton reached across her. "Oh, pardon me." He grinned as he grabbed the fruit plate.

Then he held up the *suco de goiaba.* "Can I pour you some more?" His arm brushed hers as he leaned closer with the pitcher. His foot pressed against hers under the table. Though he looked about as tired as she felt rolling out of bed so early, he was a delicious sight first thing in the morning, and for a moment, she felt more like they were on a vacation together than on a job assignment.

As they finished up breakfast, Fatima brought out a basket. "And here's the picnic you asked for." She smiled. "I know your captain. He has ten grandchildren, and he dotes on them all."

"Our captain?" Ivy turned to him.

"*Opa*. I didn't say anything." Fatima held up her hands and hurried out of the room.

"Yes, our captain. On a large sailboat that is ours for the day."

"What! We're going sailing?" She leaned closer and kissed him on the cheek, then stayed close. "How could you even know how much I love to sail?"

"I didn't. But I love to sail, like you, so it sounds like this is going to be one awesome day." It took only a small shift in the angle of his face for his lips to find hers. "Should we get started?"

"Yes." She grinned. "Thank you."

"My pleasure." His eyes searched hers. "Believe me."

She laughed, feeling a carefree happiness surround them like a lovely bubble.

They approached a marina. "We're looking for *The Menina*. She should be at the end of one of these docks."

"I see her." Ivy pointed to a tall mast with a sail still tied tight. "She's beautiful."

The boat looked like new. The deck was large. A grizzly man with tanned skin waved. "You Colton?"

"Yes, I am. Great to meet you."

"I'm Tiago. Welcome aboard. I'll be your captain and take care of everything for you. You can put your food in the galley. It's just down below. And feel free to pretend I'm not here."

"Could we help you sail?"

"Ah? A woman interested in sailing?"

"We both are." Colton led her to an opened door. "*Obrigada*, Tiago. We're just excited to get out on the water."

"With any luck, we will see some whales. The dolphins

play out there, and sometimes we see sharks." His eyes twinkled. "Which is thrilling if you are inside my large and safe boat."

"Yes." Ivy wondered at the shark population in these waters. "Looking forward to setting sail." She moved through the door that Colton held for her into a combined seating area and kitchen that was much more spacious than she thought it would be. "This is nice. And Cozy. What a great idea for a day out." She smiled, enjoying every urge she felt to kiss him in gratitude.

He took two strides. "Now, Tenderfoot. If you keep looking at me like that, we could end up anywhere."

"Why's that?"

"'Cause I won't be doing too much else besides kissing that beautiful mouth."

She laughed. "I wouldn't complain."

His gaze intensified, and he pulled her close. "Neither would I." His mouth found hers before she could respond, and it was as if they picked up right where they left off last night. But he stopped too early, kissed her again, and again, quick, meant-to-be-short moments, but he couldn't seem to stop. "Wow, you're addicting, you know that?"

She reached for his hand. "I never thought it would be like this."

"With me?"

"Right. I've always wanted to give us a try but this . . ." She shook her head.

"Okay, wait right there. Two things I want to unpack a little bit there, but let's get out on the deck and watch the boat move out across the water, and you can tell me how hot you've always thought me."

She laughed and followed him back up top to the front of the boat. "Here we go!"

Tiago had the sailboat off the dock leaving all the boats behind. Ivy stood at the very front and spread her arms out to her sides. "This is amazing! It has been way too long."

He stood behind her and rested his hands on her hips. So she leaned back into him, and his arms went around her. His chin in the small of her neck made her smile.

"Do this with me again."

She nodded. "Absolutely."

"When we're finished with this assignment down here, let's stay, get a boat, sail back home?"

She turned to face him. "What? Seriously?" A wild hope filled her. Dare she?

"I've never been more serious."

She nodded. "How about we see how things go."

"Fair enough. I don't want you getting all seasick on me."

She laughed, then she studied him. "I can't believe this. Is it really happening?"

"What happening? Our boat ride? It's definitely happening, as you can probably tell by the wind in your hair, the spray of the water, the gentle rise and fall . . . Oh, not the boat? Perhaps you mean the fact that I'm holding you in my arms and have already kissed you twice today? That part?"

"Yes, that part." She melted closer, resting her hands on his forearms. "You and I. Are we really happening?"

"Looks like it to me." He kissed the tip of her nose. "As far as we know, right? No one knows anything for sure, but so far, so good, how's that?"

She rested a hand at the side of his face. "Perfect."

He rotated his shoulders, and she turned away to watch the water. Was it her imagination, or did something not sit well with him just now? She let the thought fly away on the gorgeous breeze that tickled her neck. He would have to come to grips with whatever commitment demons he was feeling. She asked nothing more of him at the moment. She didn't know where this was going any more than he did.

"Look at that." His warm breath in her ear made her smile. His strong arm pointed off to their right.

"Is that . . ." She squinted her eyes. "A whale?"

"Not yet. But I bet we see some. That looks like a dolphin to me."

"Really? That was a big spout."

They clipped along through the water, and then right in front of them, a huge killer whale leaped up out of the water.

Ivy held her breath. Then she leaned out over the side railing, looking for any more signs of the beautiful creature.

"Wow! Would you look at that?" He pointed down at shadows in the water.

"Is that . . . a baby?" Ivy leaned over further.

"I think so."

A group of whales swam together, one smaller and sticking close to its mother swam closer to the surface, near the boat. Then the little one leaped out of the water.

Ivy stared in wonder. Colton came up behind her again, wrapping his arms around her as they peered over the water. "This is magical."

"It is." He nuzzled her neck and then placed his lips on the soft skin at the top of her shoulder. Wild goose bumps lifted the hair on her skin.

Their boat entered the open water, and the sails went up. Ivy loved the white, billowing sail as it rose to the top of the mast. When at last the ropes were tied, and the sails were up, Tiago turned their boat out of the wind and the sails filled, stretching taut against the ropes that held them back, and the boat moved across the water powered only by the wind.

She leaned back up against Colton. "It's so peaceful."

"It's the closest thing to being up close to the clouds."

"I thought riding horses was the closest thing to flying."

His low chuckle that she didn't hear but felt along her back made her smile. "Okay, so there are a few things that are the closest thing to flying."

She turned back, leaning up against the railing behind her. "Oh? And what is the other?"

His lips found hers again, and she gripped the metal railing with the happy surprise. After a moment, she nodded. "Like flying." Then she laughed. "Flyboy. Who knew."

He shrugged. "I knew. Just goes to show you that some of us are smarter than others, even if we don't prance around with clipboards and spout statistics."

"Oh, you are terrible." She shook her head. "Well, I'm happy I know now."

He leaned back against the railing at her side. "Just to be clear, what do we know?"

"That something special could happen between us." She shrugged. "That we could be so happy." She reached for his hand. "I don't know any better than you what's going to happen here, but I'm liking what we have so far."

"And to think. You were all fired-up angry at me just a month ago."

"I'm embarrassed about my letter of complaint. How presumptuous. Can I ask for it to be deleted?"

"Sure. But no harm done. We talked about it. I took it to heart. And here we are."

She searched his face, surprised. "You took it to heart?"

"Of course. The woman I most wanted to get to know,

the one I was planning on placing on my team in Brazil, was campaigning against me. I had to either fix myself or fix your perception."

"Hmm." The woman he most wanted to know? "But you never even looked in my direction. I didn't think you knew who I was before this trip."

"Oh, I knew. I remember the first time I met you. It was right before Ace pulled you in for your first assignment. You were sitting on the front row. I think you wrote down everything Amanda said."

"She's pretty awesome."

"And you wrote down some of what Ace said."

"I'm sure I did. The man is a legend in his circles."

"And Ridley." She knew where he was going with this.

"Of course I wrote down what Bear said. The man has been around a lot longer than I have."

"But . . ." He toyed with her fingers. "You didn't write down a single thing I said." He opened up a white box, pulled out two rods, and smiled. "And I knew that was just not going to work."

"What?"

"The woman I most wanted to know, thought better of my team than of me."

She didn't quite know how to respond. "I remember you cracked a lot of jokes . . ."

"But see, there's a lot people can pick up on in those jokes . . ." He paused. "And really, I'm not that person on the team. I'm not the guy with the great advice. I just do things."

She considered him. She thought about all that she'd seen him do, and she nodded. "I see that."

"You do?"

"Sure. But I do not see the fast flying, the crazy stunts, or the brave history."

"I don't understand."

"That might impress a lot of people. But I'm seeing you pick up a woman and children on the side of the road and play soccer with them all afternoon. I'm seeing you carrying laundry on your head and learning to wash clothes by hand. I'm seeing you always catching the door, looking behind you, picking up in front of you. That's what I'm seeing." She looked away, suddenly self-conscious for paying such close attention.

"You see all that? That's just . . . That's just how my mama taught me to be. You aren't a Bushman if you don't lift a hand where you can."

"Well, see, I don't think that's normal behavior for most people, and that's what I'm seeing. And it taught me to look at you in a different way."

"How am I doing?"

"At what?"

"At convincing you I'm not some crazy reckless danger to society?" He waited with a certain hesitance that was so completely endearing she wanted to kiss his face. Again.

"Oh, you're dangerous. I just can't decide if that's a good thing or not."

"Excellent." He tugged at her. "Let's get out the gear."

"Gear?"

"Sure. If we're going to catch dinner, we have to get started."

"Fishing! Awesome."

"And besides, you've got to learn a thing or two yourself before this assignment is finished."

"I do?" She stopped. "Of course I do. That's not what I

meant." She studied him, but he seemed completely engrossed in getting the line ready. "Are you gonna tell me what I have to learn?"

"Do you know how to put bait on your line?" He dragged a bucket over. What seemed like overly large minnows swam around inside.

"I don't."

"Then that, pretty lady, is what you have to learn."

She nodded. "Okay. Let's do this." She cringed a little bit when he grabbed one and put it on his hook, but she gritted her teeth and reached into the bucket for her own. It took a little longer for her to catch one. Finally, she gave up using her hands and grabbed the small net. But eventually, the poor sacrificial bait was stabbed and hanging off her hook, and she was ready to cast out.

"You ever been fishing before?"

"I have. But I'm sure I could use a refresher."

So he stood behind her, closer than necessary, but she didn't mind one bit. He held her rod and the reel and the line, and together, they brought the rod back behind her and then with a jerk, sent the bait out into the water. He reeled to lock the line in place, and then he did the same for himself, a little further down the boat.

"And now we wait."

"This is the best part of fishing." She smiled.

"Ah, you're one of those fisher types."

"What's that supposed to mean?"

"I don't know. You like to sit back and think. You probably read, thinking it's supposed to take all day to catch a fish."

"Isn't it?"

His line jerked. "Not if you do it right."

"I can't believe it." She looked at her line. It was slack in the water.

His was tugging, pulling, moving around of its own accord. The tip of his rod bent. "Oh, this is a big-un'."

She ran to him.

"You gotta watch your own line." He waved her off.

But she stuck her pole in the holders on the side of the boat and moved to his side. "It will be fine."

The fish looked like it was huge. It tugged and fought and jerked the line, moving further and further away. Colton's face was intense with concentration. For every inch the fish moved closer, it wiggled away several feet, but Colton showed no frustration, and Ivy recognized one more thing she hadn't noticed about him before. In all the time she'd known Colton, she'd not once seen him truly angry or be the one to cause contention. In fact, he was always lightening the mood, easing differences, and helping with inclusion.

Had she become so attracted to him that a few kisses could totally change her whole outlook on a person? It was more than the kisses, and she knew it.

His jaw flexed, and his arms were tight, his muscles bulging up and down his arms and across his back.

"Wow, this is tough."

He grunted. "This is a big one."

Then her pole started to bend. And then the line went out in a high-pitched whirr. "Oh, my gosh!!"

"Get it!" Colton grinned, and then his attention was immediately back on his fish.

"Like this?" She started to reel her fish in.

"Yeah, come stand by me."

She stood at his side. "This is incredible. We both caught fish!"

"Not yet, pretty lady. We have a lot of work to do, but we are going to catch them, don't you worry." He stood closer. "Now, you don't want the line to snap. I don't think it will, but you want to nudge the fish in, tease it. Trick it. As soon as it gives you a few inches, take them, but don't force it. That fish could be as big as this boat. We don't know."

She swallowed. The tugs on her line felt smaller than Colton's seemed to be. But they were nothing to discount either. Soon, she was distracted from everything around them except the constant presence of Colton at her side and the occasional touch of their arms. When her shoulders started to ache, Colton pointed to her fishing rod holder. "Put it in there. The fish won't go anywhere. Take a break."

"How did you know I was dying over here?"

"My whole upper body is on fire. I figured yours must be, too, unless you're some special gladiator muscle girl."

She shook her head. What even was that? Gladiator muscle girl? But she happily put the rod back in its place and rotated her arms. Then she moved to the edge of the railing. "Is your fish close?"

"I think so. Tell me if you see anything bump the side of the boat."

She peered down to the place where his line entered the ocean, and for a moment, everything was dark blue, but then she saw movement. A shadow. "It's huge!"

"Can you see it?" He moved to the edge, searching the water. "Oh, boy! Look at that!" He laughed and began reeling it in faster.

"What is it?"

"I can't tell." He shrugged. "But we're gonna find out."

Something splashed in the water, an almost defiant twist

of white against the blue, and then the shadow moved beneath the surface.

"What if it's a shark?" Something about seeing that dark shape below made her not want to swim anytime soon. Her line jerked, so she ran back over to the pole.

"I don't know. I guess it could be. Our bait wasn't that big, though, you know." His pole jerked especially hard, and he grunted.

She wound hers. The fish must have moved much closer since she last held it. She spun her reel until she couldn't anymore. The jerks on her line were growing stronger, and then suddenly, the line started whirring out with a high-pitched noise.

"What's happening?"

"Your fish just got a whole lot more determined."

"What do I do?" She tried to stop it with the reel, but it spun in her fingers.

Then his arms were around her, reaching for the reel, moving over her hands. He stopped the whirring and slowly started bringing it back in.

She wanted to lean back into him and close her eyes.

His own line was tugging and jerking from the rod holder.

"Thank you."

"We are not losing your fish."

She pressed her lips to his bicep that was so close to her face. "Thank you."

Chapter 15

With Ivy in his arms, the ocean all around them, the sun overhead, and two huge fish on the line, Colton laughed into the blue sky. "Whoooo!" Then he nuzzled Ivy's neck. "Ivy-Woman! This is one great day!"

She tugged on the rod. "This fish isn't going anywhere but in this boat."

"That's a girl. Okay, let's do this." He helped her, tugged some more, got some more of that line back in. Then his started to jerk more.

"Oh, mine's going a little crazy." He rushed back to his rod, moving it over to stand closer to Ivy. Then right in front of them, something banged against the boat.

"Did we do it?" Her excited squeal made him happier than he'd been in a long time.

"I think so." They peered over the edge.

A huge fish, grey topped, wiggled there. Colton spun his reel and tugged. "I'm gonna need some help here, Tiago."

"Yes, sir!" He ran as though he'd been watching the whole time, waiting for the moment. Good man.

"Help me with this?"

"We don't have a crane."

"Just use your strength. Let's get this up on deck."

Ivy stepped back and steadied herself on the railing.

"You okay?"

She didn't answer for a moment and then croaked, "He's huge. I didn't even know there were fish that big down there. I mean, sharks, sure. And whales and dolphins. But fish like that, just swimming around everywhere?" Her face went a little green, and she stared down at her rod.

"You okay, really?" He gripped the rod, but his attention was not fully on Ivy.

"Yeah. Probably." She started reeling in her fish again, but Colton made a note to bring this up again. Was she afraid?

Tiago stood at his side. When the fish left the water, the rod bent to near breaking, and with Tiago helping, they backed up and pulled the most enormous tuna he'd ever seen in his life up on deck. It flopped around, the fins sharp and pointy.

"*Opa!* Watch out." Tiago backed away.

"What are you going to do with this?" Ivy's mouth was wide open.

It jumped, totally getting air above the deck, flipping around all over the place.

She screamed and jumped back.

"I say . . . we take a picture and either let it go or donate it to Tiago here?" Colton pulled his phone out of his pocket. "Say cheese, you big old grandpa tuna!"

"Here, you get in." Tiago reached for the phone. Colton smiled. The fish was almost as long as his six-foot-four height.

Tiago grinned. "We want this fish. But I'll throw it back and drag it behind us until we get back to shore."

"You sure?" Colton gripped the man's shoulder.

"Yes. Thank you. We will eat fish for many days."

"I'm happy you'll have a use for it."

"And you and your girlfriend, you come for dinner. We cook your fresh fish."

"That would be amazing." Colton's mouth watered thinking about it. There was nothing as good as fresh-caught fish, not when it was cooked right.

Ivy was half-heartedly tugging on her own line while watching the fish. She shook her head. "I cannot believe it." She peered over the edge. "Do you think mine is that big?"

Colton reached for her rod and tugged on it. "No. Yours is smaller . . . or less of a fighter."

The line went slack, and she reeled it in like crazy. At last, the sound of a fish bumping the side of the boat seemed to give her a new burst of energy. "Yeah! Okay, let's get this guy up here." She pulled and stepped back. "I think I'm gonna need some extra muscle."

He jumped to her back again and then pulled the fish up and out of the water. As soon as its long, wide head came into view, he almost stepped back in surprise. "A hammerhead." He reached for it. It was a smaller size, still hefty, but nothing like his big monster tuna. "Would you look at that."

They flopped it up on deck, and to his surprise, Ivy reached a hand out to touch its back. "This is a beautiful fish. Hammerheads are supposed to be the good sharks, right?"

"Good, as in . . ."

"Good as in, they don't eat people." She shook her head. "Let's toss this one back."

"I agree. But not without a picture. Say cheese!" He held

up his phone and clicked a few of Ivy with her fish, which was legitimately at least half her height and possibly her weight. Then he removed the hook, and they both slid it over to the edge. "Goodbye, Hammy!" Ivy waved as it swam away.

He laughed. "Hammy?"

She wiped her hands down the front of her and then rubbed her face with her forearm.

"Feeling a little fishy?"

"Uh." She looked over the edge. "Ordinarily I might say, let's go for a swim but . . ."

"You worried about Hammy? He's long gone, and my fish, he's stuck at the back of the boat."

She shook her head. Then her face brightened. "Unless we snorkel?"

"Oh, that's a great idea. They've got fins and gear in a box on deck." He dug through the equipment, puzzling over what was bugging Ivy. "You feel more comfortable if you can see?"

She nodded. "Oh yeah. I don't think I can float there on top, knowing that somewhere below me are thousands of feet of living creatures that I can't see."

"And if you can see and there's nothing, you know that too."

"Exactly." She nodded. She stepped back inside the cabin, presumably to change into a bathing suit. He shook his head. "What a woman."

Tiago approached. "I'm going to wash down the deck." He indicated where Ivy had gone. "You going swimming?"

"I think so. Snorkeling."

"Here? *Nao, nao, Amigo*. Wait for ten minutes. I'll take you to the wreckage near a reef. She will like that much better. Colorful fish. The mystery of buried treasure . . ."

"What? That's awesome." Ivy poked her head back out, and Colton had to force himself to swallow. His mouth had just become the desert. He couldn't even answer her question. He cleared his throat. But nothing was going to work.

Ivy looked from Colton to Tiago, who finally answered for him, chuckling to himself. He explained more about his idea and where they should snorkel. While Colton watched, trying to get a grip with his realization that not only was Ivy attractive, impressive, fun, secretly daring, and full of courage, but she was smoking hot, and right now, he wasn't sure what to do about it.

She wore a black swimsuit, probably covering more of her than most girls covered in their small bikinis, but the effect was twice as sexy on her than he would have ever thought. She was stunning in every way. He struggled to keep his thoughts respectful enough so she could hear them. But he suspected she might not love his immediately masculine response to seeing her. The fact that he was already half in love and had such huge respect only added to the attraction.

"Does that sound like fun?" Ivy turned the full force of her smile on him, and all train of thought left.

"What?"

She looked at him twice before turning back to Tiago.

"I'm just gonna go change."

She waved her fingers at him, and he stepped through the door she'd just left.

"Get a grip on yourself, man." He hurried to his bag, grabbed a different pair of swim shorts, went to the back bedroom, and slipped them on.

Tiago tied the sails and used the motor to take them to the reef. "If you look straight down here, you will see the wreckage at the end of this reef. I'll drop anchor right here where it's shallow."

Ivy was the first to jump in the water. Colton had to hurry to keep up with her. He got the impression he would always be doing some hurrying to catch up with Ivy.

She swam flat on the water, her fins flipping, and her arms stretched out along her body at her sides.

Colton searched the water around her. Was he looking for sharks? Did the huge fish get him all freaked out too? He shook his head, reminding himself who was the reckless one and who the careful one. Since when did he get all worked up about possible danger?

He knew the answer. He knew what no one else did. But now wasn't the time to think about it.

Then Ivy dove. And Colton's breathing picked up. He jerked on the last flipper, yanked the mask down over his nose and eyes, and slid into the water. Immediately, he looked ahead, searching the murky water for Ivy.

An old ship down below loomed up from the depths like something out of a horror film. And at first, he couldn't see Ivy anywhere. His eyes flit about the whole area of the ocean below. She couldn't be that deep. No one had that much air. He saw a shadow below in the wreckage. A long, sinister-looking fish-like creature. His breathing picked up, and he squinted, hoping to see more clearly.

Then Ivy swam up to his side and tapped his shoulder.

He shouted in surprise inside his snorkel. Could she hear that? His heart pounded wildly. Trying to recover, he knew he was being ridiculous. What was the matter with him? He tried to make his eyes smile but wondered if instead of happy, he looked deranged. She gave him a thumbs-up and waved that he should follow her.

Her breath to prepare to go down seemed extra big, so he did the same. Then he submerged after and followed her flippers down toward the wreckage. He felt a bit calmer seeing Ivy right in front of him, and his curiosity took over. She hurried to the tallest mast, held on to the old and decaying wood, and pointed.

The boat was mostly intact. And on the opposite side, a huge turtle hovered in the water. It turned its head, stared at them for a moment, and then slowly kicked away. Ivy's hand on his arm squeezed. Then she pointed back up to the surface.

Once they were at the surface together, she treaded water and took the snorkel out of her mouth. "That was incredible. How old do you think that turtle was?"

"I don't know. At least one hundred years. They live a long time."

He pointed to the boat. "So, should we call it a day?"

She studied him for a moment. "You don't like this."

"No, it's great. What's not to like?"

"You really don't." She studied him, and he didn't like how closely she was looking or how much she could see inside him. "You're afraid?"

He looked away. "No. Come on. What's there to be afraid of?"

"Well, I was afraid of running into the fish."

"True." The depth beneath them suddenly felt very deep and unknown. He peered down into the water. Seeing everything helped. Then he lifted his face back up. "It's better when I can see. Snorkel and mask was a good call."

"Do you want to look around some more?" Her eyes told him she was ready to stay there awhile.

"Okay, sure." They put their snorkels back in their

126

mouths and moved along the surface away from the wreck and toward the reef. It had grown into the old ship and spread into a thick, green, and floral living thing, teeming with life. Smaller fish swam lazily, the kinds he saw in aquariums. He'd been snorkeling before. He'd been scuba diving once. None of this was that new. Something about being here with Ivy made it all seem . . . made him feel something he hadn't felt in a long time—vulnerable. He felt the risk to her. Of course, they were perfectly safe, he told himself. People snorkeled all the time. But he couldn't help his unease.

He ignored the depth of the water just off the ledge. And he swam closer to the reef. They went up for air and then down to the shallow reef over and over, and he began to feel more comfortable. They discovered an eel and a sea anemone that just barely opened after a long time of their patiently watching one particular ledge when a dark shadow swam overhead.

Colton almost sucked in water through his snorkel when a medium-sized shark hovered over them.

And then Ivy swam closer. She held out an underwater camera she had attached to her waist belt and must have been clicking away on it. He raced to her, yanking on her ankle and tugging her until they were hiding behind a portion of the reef, further from the shark.

When he was almost desperate for air, and he hoped the shark was far enough away, he gestured they rise, and he kicked furiously for the surface.

He waved to Tiago, who thankfully saw them right away and moved closer. When Ivy's head popped above the surface, she pulled the snorkel out of her mouth. "Colton. It's gone. It didn't even notice us or care."

"Are you out of your freaking mind?" He didn't even try

to temper his tone. "That was just plain dangerous. You trying to prove something? Because whatever it is, all you did just now is prove to me that you're dangerous. Why would anyone let you up in a plane? Someone who takes risks like that belongs behind a desk, or with that clipboard, on the ground." He turned from her toward Tiago, who had sent down a ladder. "We're getting back onboard."

She didn't respond. Her face had gone completely blank. And Colton was even more frustrated that he couldn't tell what she thought. But he didn't care anymore. He wanted them both out of the water and away from the shark.

"Boss. I think we've got company." Tiago pointed behind them.

A dorsal fin surfaced.

Colton felt battle training click on. He pushed Ivy ahead of him, nearly shoving her skyward and onto the ladder. He reached up and joined her. The fact that he hugged her with his face at her thighs didn't even register as something enjoyable. "Go! Go! Go!" He muttered.

"I'm going. Look, Flyboy. Relax."

"Says the woman who was afraid of a fish. Look, Ivy, who even are you right now? There is a shark in the water. Can you pick up the pace?"

"I think he's after the tuna."

Colton groaned. "Of course."

They climbed back on deck. And all three of them moved to the back of the boat where the fishing line seemed more slack.

"We should let him go."

The dorsal fin circled.

And then the line went taut and started moving through the water.

"I think our tuna noticed the visitor."

Tiago studied the water for only a moment and then took his knife to the line. "*Tchao*, tuna."

The fin submerged.

Then Colton turned away. "We're ready to get back."

"Right. Are we sailing? A nice sunset cruise all the way back?"

"No. Motor is fine. Look. I'm kind of tired. I'll be below."

Chapter 16

Ivy fumed, pacing on the deck while the boat picked up speed. Had she just heard him correctly? He was accusing her of reckless behavior? Warning her she didn't belong up in a plane? Flyboy? Had he heard himself? Had he looked in the mirror lately? Or seen his own flying record?

She shook her head and rested her hands on the railing. No. She couldn't bring up flying records, not when hers was what it was. But her record was maliciously and unfairly tainted. She pressed her lips together. She tried not to think about the only time she'd been disciplined and then written up in the military. It was a smudge that she would give almost anything to erase because it was so unfairly given.

She'd been on a surveillance fly-by during her deployment in Iraq. It had been a long day, and she'd been ready for home when Guido had picked up some activity on their radar. "We've got bogies."

Ivy remembered every detail of the whole mess of an experience. And she wished over and over, countless times, that she could rewrite the past. He'd deviated from their direct course back to the aircraft carrier, disobeyed orders, and turned to engage the enemy planes.

"Do not engage. I repeat. Do not engage. Return to base." The voice repeated over and over in their ears, but Guido just kept saying. "No, I got this. I know we can do this."

Ivy had shouted rules in his ears until she was hoarse.

They'd left without a skirmish. The plane moved on. And she and Guido had been soundly reprimanded for an hour, her perfect record ruined forever, and a sick dread had built in her gut. *They were going to compare her to her brother.*

"You know, your brother was one of our best pilots, as you're turning out to be, but he just couldn't keep himself in check. There is a time and place for daring bravery and a time to run from engagement."

She'd bit her tongue. She wanted to tell the commander that she had no control over Guido. She knew that no explanation would present her in any better light in her commander's eyes, so she stood, silent, while the commander said his piece. Of course he would think she was the one at fault, egging on Guido, wasn't that just what her brother would have done?

That incident had stayed with her for all other assignments, even clouding her next promotions, possibly even preventing some upward movement in rank. Some people who read her file admired Guido's gumption, and some thought it careless. But either way, she'd had to explain the situation again and again. And with each time, having to prove that she was nothing like her brother, she hated recklessness more.

But Colton had proved something about his recklessness . . . He wasn't exactly reckless, was he? He was more . . . She shrugged. She'd figure it out. If she wanted to. She frowned. But right now, she wanted nothing more to do with him. How dare he throw that back in her face! When she was willing to see past his behavior to what was going on inside him, why did he have to be so . . . quick to form opinions?

She stopped herself. Formed opinions. Exactly as she had done to him.

Her pacing quickened. They just needed to start work again. No more going out on dates, no more . . . she waved her hands around . . . whatever this was. This date.

They hardly spoke on the drive back to Fatima's. As soon as she could, she made her way to her room and spent the rest of the evening on her computer. She had some paperwork to catch up on.

Before too long, she pulled up the image of Alec, her brother. She'd studied his file. She'd gone over what went wrong with his plane. And the worst part about the whole thing was, Ivy knew how she could have saved him. She knew what she could have taught him. Top Flight included instructions on what to do in the middle of a tailspin as part of their standard curriculum. But hindsight never really helped anyone, did it?

She stared into his face. It was a picture of them together at their usual family reunion up on Lake Hagatha in New Hampshire. His arm slung across her shoulders, his carefree smile tore into her heart now as she stared into it. They couldn't afford to be carefree, could they? She considered her actions below water. Swimming toward a shark to take its picture? Probably not the best move. Probably not a risk worth taking. She closed her eyes. Tomorrow was a new day.

Hopefully a day where she wouldn't have to talk to Colton much. She needed some time to find herself again. He'd been a bad influence on her. But she could buckle down, stick to the rules, teach the pilots to do the same, and she would be back to normal safe ground.

When at last she fell asleep, it was disrupted with anxious thoughts.

Waking up after a night of ridiculous, emotional dreams involving her and Colton and dogfight after dogfight, where she was caught in a tailspin and he talked her out of it, was enough to give anyone a stiff neck. Ivy's felt as though she might never move it again.

As soon as she walked in the door, Colton called her over. "I need you up in the plane with me today."

Her breathing picked up. "What? Why?"

The group he was talking to all stopped talking and turned to look at her.

"Yes, sir. I'll go suit up." Her heart didn't know how to function anymore. She was sure of it. It pounded, and then it fluttered, and for a moment she thought it might have stopped altogether. Why? Why did she have to go up in a plane with Colton today?

Her hands shook. *Get it together, Tenderfoot.* Alec, Guido, the shark, Colton, her letter criticizing his recklessness, everything came flooding back to her in a great wave. What was the problem here? She reached a hand out to the wall. The other clutched her stomach. The world seemed to wobble, so she closed her eyes. She started to sink to the floor as darkness crowded in.

Then strong arms encircled her. And Colton's voice. "I've got you." He pulled her close then lifted her in his arms.

She leaned her head up against his shoulder.

He carried her to an empty room that looked like it might be a storage room of some kind. Then he placed her on a chair, opened a bottle of water and offered it. "What's this all about?"

His eyes were wide and caring.

She took the offered water and drank about half of the bottle before she faced him again. "I'm a mess."

"I can see that. You wanna explain to me what's going on?" His words sounded harsh, but his eyes were full of fear, and concern, and possibly . . . love?

She blinked. Then she saw caring, certainly, probably not love.

"I—" What was she to say here? That she was all worked up about her brother and her record and that Colton made her crazy?

"I—I'm sorry I swam toward the shark."

He studied her for a few moments, long enough that she couldn't even begin to guess what was going through his mind. "That's it?"

"What do you mean that's it?"

"That's why you went white when I told you that you were flying today? That's why you almost passed out in the hall? Because of the shark?"

She shook her head. "Honestly, I'm not totally sure what's wrong with me."

He studied her some more, and then his maddening, slow smile took over his face, and she was caught up in it, watched it, and felt its magic hover around inside.

"What?" She returned his amused and caring expression with a growing smile of her own. "What is so entertaining?" She crossed her arms.

"Well, for one, I don't know if I can forgive you."

"What?" She was beginning to sound like a child on repeat.

"That kind of reckless behavior that puts other pilots at risk."

She groaned. "And that's the other thing."

"Ah, so there's more."

"Of course. I'm not sitting up all night with terrible dreams because of the shark."

"Well, I would have been." He eyed her. "Just saying."

"I'm sorry for that letter of complaint I wrote."

"So, you're having remorse?"

"Yes, no. Not really, no. I'm just sorry about the letter because I was wrong."

"Don't worry about that. We all knew you were wrong."

"You did?" She wasn't sure how she felt about her opinions being discounted.

"Don't get me wrong. I was struck . . . I considered your opinions. I may have toned down my original introductions to the pilots. I see how I'm coming across."

"Hmm." She fidgeted. "And I want to tell you about my brother."

"Can we talk about it up in the air?"

She shuddered.

"What's the matter?"

"I don't know. I think I'm having a relapse of stress surrounding the actions of Guido."

"Guido? The guy who nearly lost his life going after some bogies over Iraq?"

"Yes."

"You were up in that plane?"

She nodded.

"Now that is the first bit of sense I've heard you say in this whole conversation."

"No, hold on. Me apologizing has lots of sense in it."

"True. True. I'm not knocking your heartfelt, beautiful apologies." He shook his head. Then he tucked a stray hair behind her ear. "But that whole mess with Guido, that explains a whole heck of a lot of stuff."

"Does it?"

"Yes. For example, how a woman as daring and exciting as you, one who swims toward sharks, can be so uptight about my maneuvers. Someone who herself flies just as carefree and, dare I say, reckless?" He nodded, obviously just getting started. "Who takes unknown horses over jumps without a single bit of preparation. Reckless."

"We need a different word."

"Yeah. Awesome. That's what it is. When I do it."

"Fair enough."

"But you. You . . ."

"There's more. Have you ever heard of Alec Halstead?"

He started to shake his head, but then she added, "Venom."

His eyes bulged. "Halstead."

"He was my brother."

His hand went to his forehead. "Of all the things to not know. Does Ace know?"

"Yes, and Amanda."

"But not me."

"I try to hide it from most people."

"And I'm most people."

"You were, yes."

He seemed to sit up a little taller. "But not anymore?"

"I don't know, Colton. I'm freaking out about having to

fly again. I don't want to spin into this fear cycle. It took me six months to get out of it." She gripped his sleeves. "Help."

"Hey. I'm here. We're not gonna let that happen to you. Because look at me."

She lifted her lashes.

"I'm gonna be there. I'm gonna take care of you. And someone needs to talk the other pilots down. We've got a few freaking out up there, and I need you. I need your voice, your experience. Come on, Ivy. You and I can do anything up there. Trust me."

She sucked in a breath. And that was the crux of it. Did she trust him? His eyes begged her to give him a shot. His hand laced his fingers with hers. But he didn't say anything more. And maybe it was his patience that did it, but as she searched his face, she knew she wanted to trust him. She stared deeply into his eyes, and then her gaze moved down his face to his lips. Before she could think of anything else, she was clinging to him, her arm flung around his neck, her lips covering his in a desperate plea. A plea that turned into confidence almost immediately. A deep core of warmth and peace filled her just as a new crazy desire raced through her blood, and the combination was intoxicating, as high as anything she'd ever felt, as adrenaline-pounding as the craziest stunt. She was in love with Colton Bushman, and she trusted him.

Her mouth stretched into a smile. And she nodded. "I trust you." She smiled through new misty eyes. "I totally trust you. You. Colton. Flyboy, the fastest pilot anyone's heard of, the guy crazy enough to do the things you've done, and I trust you."

He pressed his lips to hers one more time, a kiss filled with promise, and then he stood. "Good, because we have a plane to fly."

His hand that held hers was solid, sure, and she knew that together, she felt strong. Together, she'd even approached a shark. Together she would be able to face her old fear again and go up in the air. She'd gone up with him once before. That helped. This new trust would get her through.

Chapter 17

Colton still wasn't completely sure what went down with Ivy in the hall, but he knew he would trust her, just like she'd said she trusted him. He was going to trust that she would pull through whatever demons were after her. Had her news surprised him? Shocked him, more like.

Guido. She had been up with the idiot Guido. This should have been in her file. Maybe it was. For everyone but him to see.

And Venom. He whistled. *Venom*. That guy was infamous. Colton had a secret respect for the dude; it took a lot of nerve to do what he did. Dumb nerve, but nerve.

He tried not to look at Ivy with new eyes, but he couldn't help it. She had fire burning through her. He knew that from her kisses. His own blood sizzled just thinking about her. But it was a different kind of fire. A different spark.

They went through inspections. Tested their instruments. And then climbed up into the plane.

"We have to shoot them down." Colton adjusted their instruments.

"I thought you said they need some help."

"This is what they need the most."

"Okay." Her voice sounded weak, tentative.

He counted to three, knowing what she was thinking. Then she said, "But I think it might be better if they feel successful."

"Not these guys. They think they already know everything, and they have a chip on their shoulders about the women in the group." He rotated his shoulders. "One of them was making some comments. Made our women pilots uncomfortable."

"They reported him?" Ivy was silent long enough Colton guessed she was fuming. "Let's shoot them down as fast as anyone's ever been shot down. What's the record?"

He chuckled. "That's the spirit. But now, humor me a little bit. We've got to toy with them first."

Her frustrated sigh while he finished running the inside pre-flight inspection made him smile. In truth, he wanted these two pilots to succeed. They were by far the best pilots of their group, but they had a few lessons to learn before they would be well and truly safe. Before their county could trust them to fly their most expensive assets.

And he wanted them to learn these lessons today before they went any further.

They burst into the sky. As soon as he saw blue all around him, his life shifted, and more started to make sense. Ivy. He liked her there with him. He should just tell her that. His eyes lifted to their monitors. She was watching him.

He pulled off his mask and smiled. "I like you here."

"Here, here?"

"Yeah, flying with me. Anything with me, actually."

"I like me here too."

He nodded.

His instrument dial beeped. Someone had their guns aimed and locked on target.

"Oh, no, you don't." He dove. "Ivy, things are going to get a little reckless."

"Oh, stop. That's not reckless. That's child's play."

"Right on. Do I have your permission to show these two what real flying looks like?"

"Yes, you do. Now, go get them."

"Whoohoo!" He dove the other direction, spun in the air, pushed on the air brakes, dropped behind the other plane, put them in his sights, and shot a pretend missile.

He let what had just happened to them sink in, and then he turned on the radio. "Thank you, Firebrand and Burger. Send up the next two."

As soon as his radio was off, Ivy called out, "How fast was that?"

"I don't even know. That was way too close, though. We can't let them catch us off-guard again." He eyed her in the monitor. "Can't blame a guy. When a hot girl just admitted she wants to spend time with me, I got a little distracted."

They flew the rest of the day, taking down one pilot after another as fast as they possibly could.

"Oh, boy. This is going to be one rough day for these pilots."

They made their way back to the classroom. "I think I'm going to leave this to you." Colton held out his fist for her to bump.

"Why me?"

"You know what they did wrong. You know how we exploited it. I want you to drill into them that mistakes happen, but some mistakes are dumber than others."

She nodded. "I can do that."

"Excellent. Then I'm going to come in and drill it in them again."

They did just as he suggested. And it took more out of Ivy than she thought it would. She'd gone to great lengths to show each pilot specifically what he needed to improve upon, and in some cases, it didn't go down as well as she would like, so it had taken more energy. But by the time she and Colton were both done with them, each pilot had had a harsh reality lesson and, at the same time, hope for their future flying ability.

THE NEXT MORNING, Colton watched Ivy run out the front door with air pods in her ears and wearing running shorts. Something about that sight, watching her check her watch and move off into the misty morning, solidified a couple of things in his mind. One being that he knew he wanted Ivy in his life. What he'd said up in the plane, he'd meant it. He liked Ivy with him. He wanted her in his life. Always? Maybe. That thought floored him. He'd never once wanted a woman in his life forever.

Omar knocked on his bedroom door. "Hey, man. You got a minute?"

"Sure thing."

When Omar closed the door behind him, Colton's interest piqued. "What's on your mind?"

"It's the guys."

"Who?"

"Antonio, Burger, Firebrand, Ferdinand, all of them. They aren't sure we're giving them what we said we would."

"What's that supposed to mean?" Colton didn't like the sound of that.

"Don't get all up in arms with me. I'm just passing along something I'm noticing. They're all complaining that most of this stuff they could learn anywhere and that they already learned it from their own government."

"Brazil has a pilot training program?"

"An in-classroom with some time in a jet. Similar to what we're doing."

"Do you agree with them?"

"No. But here's where I think it's coming from. You guys sell this training as out of the box, as touting real flight experience. You have a reputation. When Flyboy is coming, there's a certain expectation."

Colton started to bristle. He tried to keep his face passive. He needed to understand where the disappointment was coming from, and if he got all defensive, Omar might shut down or temper his comments.

"I mean, you haven't even done the move yet."

He looked away. He'd been flying carefully. He told himself he was doing what he would do no matter what, that the pilots weren't ready to be trying anything more advanced, but he knew he'd just been altering his behavior because Ivy was watching. He could just imagine her reaction if he were to invert a plane for no other reason except to show off to the pilots. But it wouldn't be just to do that. He'd always told himself and anyone else who cared to listen that understanding those more advanced maneuvers could save your life someday. And Omar had a point, he was doing everyone a disservice by not including at least a demonstration by now in their training.

"What do you think I should do?"

Omar eyed him for a moment. "Don't fly with Ivy in your head."

Colton grunted. How was that even possible? She was always in his head. But especially when he flew. It was her letter about him. And then they'd talked about it. He realized he'd been holding back when he flew, knowing he'd see her as soon as he stepped back into the classroom. And that meant he had not included anything that he would normally have by now: some of his more advanced flying that Ivy might consider dangerous.

"You want to go up with me tomorrow?"

"Yep." Omar grinned. "You gonna do the move?"

"Sounds like I have to."

"All right! I can't wait to hear them talk about it after. They're going to die, plain and simple. It's one thing to hear about the move, but seeing it, even on a radar monitor, that'll shut their mouths, that's for sure."

"You did great telling me. Thanks."

They bumped fists, and Omar left.

Colton was left wondering how he could send Ivy on some errand into town tomorrow, anywhere she wouldn't see him doing the same moves that her brother and Guido had been guilty of. Colton sat in the nearest chair. What was the difference between him and Alec? Besides the fact that Alec had messed up and the plane had gone into a tailspin, Colton hoped his own actions had been more merited. He hoped that he had flown the way he did at times with good reason, that he was the hero his medals said he was. But a part of him knew that he loved to see what the planes could do. Did he choose to use more reckless maneuvers when other ones would work fine or even better? Who knows? But one thing was certain. If he didn't start delivering on some of the instructions for these more challenging options, Ace was going to start hearing some of the complaints Omar got. And maybe not just Ace. Word of mouth was everything in this business.

Besides all that, Colton hated letting them down. What were they saying? That he wasn't all that they'd heard? That he flew scared? He shook his head. He'd stop that talk right in its tracks before it could go anywhere else.

And then hope that Ivy understood it needed to be done.

Chapter 18

Ivy watched Omar and Colton leave together with helmets on their hips. And she tried not to feel like she'd been replaced. Of course Omar would get to fly with Colton sometimes too. She'd just come to think of herself as his co-pilot. They were to watch the flight patterns and activity today. Colton wanted them to analyze what was happening in the air.

They turned on the monitors on the far wall. A large screen lit. When Colton's face filled one half of it, she could only laugh at his expression.

The classroom quieted when Colton turned on his radio. "Hello, pilots. We are going to have some real dogfight action this morning. But unlike other in-flight training, these guys are going to stay in the air even if we get a tone."

"So they're gonna get hit over and over and over." Antonio laughed, and the rest of the class joined in.

"If you pay attention, you just might be able to get a tone on us after we're through here." Ivy sat, facing the screens. It would be tougher for them with only the two planes, but it was possible. Especially after she and Omar and Colton left. They could work on the things they'd been taught, every day if they wanted.

They'd been flying for five minutes, Ivy explaining all the different things Colton was doing to evade Antonio. The more Ivy talked about him, pointing out his moves, the greater respect she had for him. "See that last move? He could have chosen any number of things to use to get away, but he chose the simplest, the safest."

Two of the pilots rolled their eyes.

"Do you have a problem with safe and simple?"

"No, ma'am." His words said one thing, but his smirk said something else entirely.

And for the first time since her flight with Guido, she was mildly tempted to show off a little. How easy it would be to put this pilot in his place. But she shook her head. "Look, Firebrand. Something we hope you learn with us is that there is a time and place for the more advanced moves. But if a simple one will suffice, then that is the better choice."

Colton's voice came on. Ivy turned up the volume. "So now you have probably heard us say that there is a time and place for the more advanced moves. Today is that time and place."

The pilots clapped. "About time." One of them held up his phone.

"No recording, please." Ivy waved at his device.

He grumbled but put his phone back in his pocket.

The other plane came closer to Colton than was necessary, and Ivy cringed. But Colton responded immediately, of course. His reflexes were lightning fast. They dove away, with a triple sideways spin.

The pilots all around her cheered.

Then Colton took the plane straight up into the sky, something she herself had done their first day flying in Brazil. He continued his evasive techniques, getting tone over and over again on the other plane.

"Come on, boys. Let me see what you've got. See if you can shoot down the Fly."

Ivy found herself half rooting for Colton and half for the other pilots. Usually, by the end of their training, at least one of the pilots could beat them in a dogfight. She thought it evidence of a truly superior program, and she was proud of that. But something about Colton's challenge didn't sit well, and Ivy hoped that it wouldn't happen today.

Then the other pilots did one of Colton's signature moves, his forward roll, but they weren't able to pull out of it as quickly, and they free fell in a spin for a moment longer than they should have.

Ivy sucked in her breath. "Pull out, Antonio. Pull out."

They did, but the room went quiet.

"That's very lucky." Ivy indicated Antonio's image and his heavy breathing from the sound.

"That was something, Antonio." Colton pulled up beside him. Ivy could see his plane next to Antonio's in the air. "Maybe you were trying something like this?"

"No," Ivy murmured under her breath.

But Colton dove and completed the same forward spin, whipping his plane behind theirs and getting tone.

"That was not necessary," Ivy began.

But Colton's voice interrupted. "Not necessary but fun." He laughed. "And one day, it could very well be the most necessary thing you ever do." He twisted off to the side. "Here's another unnecessary move that could save your life."

Ivy couldn't tell what he was doing exactly at first, but as the plane rolled, she was back with Guido, and then she was flying with her brother like she had wished for so many years. "What are you doing, Flyboy?"

He didn't answer. He spun again and then Omar's voice —"Pull up, Colton. We're gonna be too low."—dried her throat out to one big desert. She cleared her throat.

"Pull up, Fly. Pull up." In her mind, Alec was pilot, and then Colton, then Guido. And she felt sick with dread. "No."

But the plane started spiraling out of control. She saw nothing else around her. Every part of her brother's death replayed in her mind as she watched Flyboy perform the same maneuver. Would she lose them both right now? For a dumb show-off maneuvering?

Right as they entered the height from which they could not return, Colton somehow managed to get control and sent his plane back up to previous height.

The classroom broke out into cheering.

Flyboy's voice and his salute brought out more cheers. "Let's take her down, gentlemen."

The pilots ran out the door and down to the hangar. They cheered Colton and Omar all the way back to the classroom. Ivy didn't know how to feel. Except betrayed. Somehow, after telling Colton about the two ghosts of her past, she thought that he'd learned something from them. That out of respect for her feelings, he'd stay away from the very thing that had killed her brother.

Even as she thought it, she knew it was ridiculous. He couldn't fly differently to spare her feelings. But then again, hadn't he just proved her point? He was reckless and dangerous and had almost just died because of it, nearly bringing down a billion-dollar plane with him.

She stepped out of the classroom. This was not her place.

Colton had some things to teach those other pilots, and he was the one to do it. They didn't need Ivy's more cautious opinions right now, nor did they want them. And she couldn't watch while Colton demonstrated the very thing that had killed Alec.

She slipped out of the hangar and called Fatima. "Is there someone who can come get me?" Her breathing was coming faster, her head starting to spin. She knew she was freaking out. Probably hyperventilating but . . . there was nothing she could do about it. And that scared her most of all.

By the time she was back at Fatima's, she knew she could no longer stay. She would leave the rest of the training to Omar and Colton. If Top Flight didn't understand, then maybe . . . She choked on the thought. Maybe it was time for her to give up planes. Nothing she could do would ever bring back her brother. She wasn't saving lives or stopping the same behavior in other pilots. The very man she'd . . . fallen for thought it important to know how to be dangerous. Flying was dangerous. She'd known that when she entered the Air Force.

She packed her things. Her ride would pick her up and take her to the airport before Colton and Omar returned. Fatima's arms tight around her gave her some sense of comfort, but the predominant desire was to run. She no longer belonged in this world of flying and danger, and she didn't want to. Perhaps that feeling should have been freeing, but she could only feel a sense of dread about never seeing Colton again . . . but at the same time, she felt a fear of having to face him.

Her car came. The airport was closer than she remembered. And before too long, she was flying away from Brazil toward Boston.

Chapter 19

Colton returned to the house, looking for Ivy. She hadn't returned any of his calls. He knew she couldn't be too happy with him, but he'd done the right thing. The pilots had been as attentive as ever. They had even learned from his spin out of control. He'd not known if he would pull out of that, and he told them as much point-blank. He talked about what you do in situations like that, what you can try, and how you hope something will work. He talked about plane malfunctions and when to use certain maneuvers. It was one of the most productive and important days of the Top Flight training. And even if Ivy thought it hard to see, days like today were part of the reason he stayed with Top Flight, were why he thought it important in the first place.

But now he hoped to make it right. "Ivy!" he peeked his head in the kitchen. "Hello, Fatima. Do you happen to know where Ivy is?"

She clucked, and then his heart sank. "She's probably halfway home by now, *querido*."

He checked his phone again for a message, something, from her.

"I think she left you a note? She said to tell you and Omar not to worry. Something had come up, and she needed to be home."

Colton knew exactly what had come up. He just didn't know if she forgave him or if she left in angry rebellion. Was she still a part of Top Flight? Were they still . . . friends, at least?

He and Omar ate dinner, but they were both quiet. Finally, Omar downed his juice and said, "I'm sorry she left, dude."

"Me too, man. But maybe it's for the best. We can finish out what we need to with these pilots. And she won't have to be disturbed by it." He wished she'd just see things his way. But he also understood that today especially, had to have been a trigger for her. He didn't know exactly what move had sent Alec into a tailspin, but Colton knew watching his plane spin out of control had to have been extremely difficult for her. His eyes met Omar's. "I'm just glad we were able to spin out of that alive." He raised his own juice cup. Omar lifted his empty one. "Here's to being alive."

"Cheers."

That evening was lonely. Omar went out to play football with the local guys, but Colton wanted to make some phone calls.

Ivy didn't answer. His message probably sounded too formal. But he didn't want to sound too pleading.

Ace picked up on the first ring. "So Ivy left."

"Did she call you?" Colton asked.

"Yeah. Well, she called Amanda."

"And? Did she say why?"

"She's trying to decide if she still wants to be a part of Top Flight."

Colton whistled. "I really did a number on her."

"You know about her brother?"

"Yeah."

"Give her some time."

"So I think we are good down here without a third. But it is helpful to have another person in the classroom now and then."

"Do you want me to send someone?"

"Is Ivy really not coming back?"

"She didn't indicate she was. You'd be the best one to guess at that."

"I've got nothing. The woman is more a mystery to me now than ever. Right when things were getting good. Right when I thought we might go someplace . . . she takes off at the first sign of danger. Ace, dude. We're fighter jet pilots. This has never been a safe job."

"Do you love her?"

He let out a huge breath, slowly. "I think so?" The thought hit him. His own words echoed around in his brain. "I miss her." He laughed. "Omar is great, but it's not the same."

Ace laughed. "Go visit. When you're finished down there, take a few weeks in Boston or wherever she ends up."

"Good call. Maybe don't put me on the next round of assignments. I'll take the last half of the year off."

"You're coming back, though, right?"

"Of course, dude. What else would I do?"

"Get married and stay safe so your wife can feel comfortable."

He didn't deny the thought had occurred to him. But he

couldn't imagine a life without Top Flight, even if only on a smaller scale. And honestly, he couldn't imagine Ivy would ever want to marry him.

They'd set it up so that more people could head missions. The board could relax a bit more. Ivy was one they relied on for that. They'd been talking about sending her on her own next. "Dude, sorry I might have wrecked our best pilot."

"You didn't wreck her. She's got some things to work through. You just pushed them to the surface. Unless she figures this out, she's more of a danger than you are."

They hung up. He sent another text to Ivy and then turned off his phone.

WORKING with the pilots was now easier than ever. They were excited. They learned quickly. They studied harder. Colton and Omar pushed them through the whole next month without showing them any more advanced moves. Colton found it more rewarding than ever. And if Ivy had been there, this would be his favorite assignment of all of them. But her absence burned a hole in his peace of mind.

He still checked his phone every day for any news from Ivy. She'd texted him one time. "*I explained everything in my letter. I need to think through some things. Good luck on the rest of the training.*"

In her letter, she'd basically told him what he already knew. She had been majorly triggered by his spin out. Living through that moment in real time, thinking she might lose someone she cared about, had brought a lot of things home to her, and she had emotionally cracked. She hoped to heal enough to figure out her place in the piloting world. She wanted to be a part of Top Flight, and she was thankful for their patience. Mostly it was an impersonal letter about her job. But at the end, she said something that gave him a sliver of hope. "We have something special. I don't want to lose that. But I'm not sure how to keep it."

That made sense to him. But he didn't know how to keep things either, not if she was going to be living in fear of his work.

He and Omar worked well together. He'd be recommending that the man lead his own team soon. Maybe in a few more missions. He'd wait to hear what the others thought of him.

The remaining months went by faster than he thought they would. When they were at last finishing up, Colton wasn't sure where to go. He had an apartment near Ace's in Arlington, Virginia. He had his parents' place in Texas where he could ride his horse, or . . . he could go track down Ivy in Boston.

She hadn't answered him when he'd reached out to see about when he could come to visit. Ace was not anywhere near his place in Arlington. But as he went to buy tickets to Dallas, he couldn't do it. So he bought tickets to Boston instead. If she didn't want to see him, he'd catch a Cubs game. He'd been a fan for years.

Saying goodbye to Fatima and the guys was harder than he thought. She kissed his cheeks twice and held his face in her soft hands. He hugged her close. "I'm going to miss you and your special home. Thank you for taking such good care of us."

"You come back. And bring some more of your American pilots."

"I'll try."

He'd stopped by the home of the nanny he'd found on

the side of the road with her employer's children. She had moved out of that family home and found a job in another, someone Fatima knew. She seemed happy. He'd brought treats to the kids and the men who played soccer on that strip of dirt nearby. Colton was going to miss Brazil. A special people.

The pilots were ready. A few of them were safely doing more advanced moves. And even though Colton was never sure why Brazil wanted a trained group of fighter jet pilots, they now had one. Another Top Flight assignment completed with success.

HIS PLANE LANDED in Boston in the early morning. He made his way to a hotel room and then showered before heading to the address he had on file for Ivy.

When he knocked, a man answered the door. "May I help you?" He was young, could be considered good looking by some, dressed in a suit. Colton tried not to frown. "Hey, I'm a co-worker of Ivy's. Is she here?"

"Ivy Hatfield? No. I'm subletting. She hasn't lived here in a couple of months."

"Do you know where she is?"

The man studied him for a moment and then flat out lied. "No, I don't."

"You sure? 'Cause last time I saw her she said she wanted to touch base again."

"Then I'm sure you can get her on her cell phone."

"Fair enough." He lifted his phone to his ear. When voicemail began, he said, "Hey, Ivy. I'm standing in front of your apartment, talking to your new tenant. Just wondering where you are. Give me a call." He pocketed the phone.

The guy shrugged. "Good luck." Then he closed the door.

But Ivy never called him back. Colton stuck around long enough to see two Cubs games and to do the historical walking tour of Boston by himself. He knew the hotel staff by name before he finally gave up and flew home to Dallas.

Chapter 20

Ivy tugged on the sail rigging. The wind caressed her face and arms. The sun felt delicious on her slightly chilled skin. The water stretched in every direction, and she drank in the quiet. She loved the first moments with the motor turned off, and the only sounds the wind rustling the sails. She'd seen the last of the Cape Cod shoreline yesterday. Now she set her sights on Nantucket. She'd purchased a tiny run-down cottage that claimed a piece of waterfront and a dock to tie her boat. And that's where she wanted to spend the rest of her summer. She'd purposely bought no WiFi. Her phone sat turned off in a drawer down in her cabin. And she had begun a strong course of true healing. She'd met with a counselor who thought her perfectly normal but gave her so many useful ways to handle her triggers, to help her safely fly again if she wanted.

So far, she didn't want to. Which was odd. Even during her first episodes after the incident with Guido and her brother's death, a part of her always still wanted to fly. But not now. Now she was feeling strangely and happily fulfilled out on the water.

She felt close to Colton.

And strangely, she'd acquired a new fascination with sharks.

The boat sped up as the wind filled the sails. "All right!" She laughed. For the most part, she was completely satisfied with her new solitude.

Except for this itch that wouldn't go away, a consistent tugging and emptiness in one part of her heart that she now recognized belonged to Colton. But she didn't know what to do about it.

She knew he texted and called her often. Sometimes she listened to his messages. Sometimes she didn't. She read all of his texts. They were short, simple, reaching out to be able to talk to her.

Maybe she would be ready soon. She admitted to herself that this whole sail and summer in Nantucket would be much better with Colton than it would be alone. But what? They weren't married. They weren't even dating.

She'd been out on the water like this for months. She stopped to restock her supplies. And then she learned she could anchor offshore and pay for grocery delivery and trash pick-up. That had been a game changer. She had filled her Kindle before she left and had a stack of books to read down in her cabin. This boat was her best purchase yet. She hoped her cabin in Nantucket would be equally enjoyable.

She smiled up into the sun. She would sail to a known sandbar, drop anchor, and then finish her journey to her new island home the next day. A part of her wanted to start up the portable WiFi she'd brought for emergencies. What had

Colton said recently? Did he still want to see her? He'd finished their Top Flight assignment and was undoubtedly home from Brazil by now.

The idea persisted for long enough that as soon as she was safely anchored, she booted up her WiFi, used the generator for electricity for the first time in a long time, and checked her phone messages.

She laughed out loud with pleasure at his message when he was standing in front of her apartment. So, he'd come all the way to Boston? She dialed his number. Her hands shook a little, but mostly she just felt happy anticipation.

But the call went through to voicemail. "Hey, this is Colton. I'm back on my horse for the next month or two. If I don't get back, Pepper says hi."

She almost didn't leave a message, but then she said simply, "Hey. Miss you."

She turned off the phone, shut down the WiFi, and turned off the generator. Falling asleep to the sound of waves lapping and the gentle rocking of her boat was one of heaven's greatest gifts.

The next morning, helicopter blades woke her. She sat up, wiping sleep from her eyes. Her heart flipped a couple of times. She hurried up on deck and squinted into the early morning sun toward the sound.

A government-issued bird approached. She could tell it wasn't going to be a flyby. She moved to the railing, wondering. And hoping.

When it got close enough, she laughed into the wind at Colton's face, leaning out the opened door. She waved back.

Then he held the intercom radio to his mouth. Over the loudspeaker, she could make out his words over the sound of the blades whipping in the wind, keeping the helicopter hovering slighting above her position. "Can I drop down?"

She grinned, thinking for a moment, then nodded and waved him to come.

He didn't wait another second before jumping down into the water.

She lowered the ladder over the side and ran for a towel.

When his face popped up, water cascading off of him, his hair beautifully mussed up, he said, "I heard someone missed me?"

"It's the strangest thing."

He climbed out and walked to her outstretched towel. He ran the towel through his hair and looked around. "All this beauty to look at, and you missed a sorry cowboy pilot?"

She stepped closer. "It's like everything I do is missing something."

His eyes lit. Then he stood close enough she could see his skin underneath his wet shirt. She could feel the heat between them, even though he was drenched with the cold northeastern ocean water. She stepped even closer, his wet clothes brushing against her dry ones.

"You'll get wet." His voice was low, husky, inviting.

She wrapped her arms around him, immediately drenched through. "Thanks for coming."

"I've learned something over these last few months without you."

"Oh yeah? What's that?"

He got as close as he could without actually kissing her. She felt the cold from the ocean off his mouth. She felt the puffs of his breath on her lips. "Everything I do is missing something too." Then he pressed his lips to hers, capturing her in a great love that seeped through everything between them. Tendrils of happiness, joy, and completion filled in all the lonely gaps, and at once, everything that had been missing all these months was now found. She wrapped her hands tighter around his shoulders.

His fingers spread, and his palms slid across her back, lowering down to her waist. He pulled her closer, and she tried to capture more of his mouth, more of him.

After a moment she hoped would never end, she noticed the area around them had once again grown quiet. "I think you lost your ride." She mumbled against his lips.

"Hmm?"

"They left you." She pulled away. "Is that a problem?"

"Not for me." He searched her eyes. "But, they are ready to come back and get me whenever you think it's time to give me the boot."

"How about a sail to Nantucket and a fixer-upper project this summer?" Her eyes sparkled.

"As far as invitations go, that is the best I've heard in years." He cradled her closer. "I love you, Ivy. In case that isn't clear. I love you. And I'm sorry I scared you. And if I could, I would keep you blissfully safe and unscared for the rest of your life."

His words flowed through her, igniting her insides with the power of his words. "I love you too. And I wouldn't stress too much about keeping me safe. I should tell you. I swim with sharks now."

The shock on his face, the horror of it in his mind, almost made her laugh, but she knew what it felt like to worry for the safety of the person you loved. "But I won't tell you about it if you don't tell me about whatever you do."

He looked like he might complain or have another opinion about her shark swimming, but instead, he just nodded. "Deal. That seems fair."

"Good, now, let's get you out of that shirt."

His grin grew. "I love the sound of that."

But she just laughed. "Then you can help me dock her. I was wondering how to do that part by myself anyway."

"Happy to be of service." He stepped through the door leading down to the berths. Then he poked his head back out. "Do you have anything else I can wear onboard?"

"Fortunately, not really." She laughed.

Then when he turned a particularly adorable shade of red, she had some mercy on him. "Feel free to stay shirtless, but if you look in the second berth, you should see some clothes that might fit."

"Do I want to know why you have men's clothing on board?"

"No."

He nodded and left it at that.

She grinned to herself. The fact that her cousins had borrowed the boat last week could remain a mystery for at least the next twenty minutes.

As she prepared the sails to make the rest of their journey, she let the peace and calm from his arrival seep into the deepest parts of her. Colton made everything better. He filled in the empty spots, and she knew she loved him. Perhaps they could make it work, maybe they could be together, and she might even be able to take another assignment with Top Flight. But she was pretty sure she never wanted to work with him again. It would just be easier that way. Could this be her future? With Colton at her side? She knew this summer would help her know. But as he poked his head back out, dressed in dry clothes, his smile larger than she'd ever seen it, she loved him even more, and she already knew he was her future.

—Read all books in the Top Flight Fighter Pilot Romance Series. Click HERE

Read all books by Sophia Summers

Read all the books in The Swoony Sports Romances
Hitching the Pitcher
Falling for Centerfield
Charming the Shortstop
Snatching the Catcher
Flirting with First
Kissing on Third

Her Billionaire Royals Series:
The Heir
The Crown
The Duke
The Duke's Brother
The Prince
The American
The Spy

Read all books by Sophia Summers

The Princess

Her Billionaire Cowboys Series:
Her Billionaire Cowboy
Her Billionaire Protector
Her Billionaire in Hiding
Her Billionaire Christmas Secret
Her Billionaire to Remember

Her Love and Marriage Brides Series
The Bride's Secret
The Bride's Cowboy
The Bride's Billionaire

Her Single Holiday Romances
Taming Scrooge

About the Author

Billionaires, Royals, Marriages of convenience, Cowboys, and Athletes. Sounds exciting, doesn't it?

Sophia Summers is an award winning author who just wants to relax a little and enjoy a great beach read. She lives in a quiet southern town brimming with an extra dose of hospitality and a whole lot of charm.

She writes historical romance under a different name. You can follow her on http://www.sophiasummers.com. You can join her Newsletter at her webpage or if from an ebook, JOIN HERE .

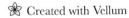

Made in the USA
Coppell, TX
19 June 2021

57748613R00098